Cheerleaders, Coaches, Comrades & Champions

Building the Team that Builds You!

By

Andrea L. Humphrey

Dedication

Dr. Sharon Rabb

Thank you for teaching me how to be a cheerleader, a coach, a comrade, and a champion to those God has entrusted to my influence. You helped me believe again, and for that I am eternally grateful. I live to honor the legacy you poured into me, and I look forward to seeing you again in glory.

Forever One of Yours

Acknowledgement

First and foremost, I thank God for the blessing of being trusted to write, teach, and speak all over the world. I am because God is.

I would like to thank the first Cheerleaders in my life, my parents, Lillian Jones, Vern Carradine, and Toni Adams, my husband, Charles Humphrey Jr, my amazing daughters, Lauryn & Sydney Humphrey, and my siblings, Tracy, Gina & Stephon. I am grateful for my church H.O.P.E. 's House Christian Ministries (especially P. Ray, Ms. Bri, Kelvin, Will, Reens, Styles, Tameika, Melvin, Taylor, and the leadership teams) and the grace you extend to me to pastor and cast vision for the house. To Pastor Jon DeCuir, Dr. Ronn Elmore, Pastor Albert Tate, Dr. Dani Falcioni, Elder Claybon, Marc2, Sekou, Dex, Merea, Tristan, and Elena, who have served as Coaches in a variety of ways, thank you for your expertise and the grace you have extended me. My Comrades (and confidants), Tish, Eric, Tiffany, Adrienne, Wendy, Dr.Tamika, Felicia, Cheryl, Marcel, Val, Eman, Karen, Syretta, Tracey, Shunna, Alex, Anthony, Allison, Bonnie, Dez, Pastors James and Nicole White, Aladrian, Pastors OL & Karelyn Kelley, Pastor Hilda, Pastors Vincent and Felica Campbell, Ndume, Pastor Brenda, Niki & Kevin B.

Finally, I want to thank the many Champions who made this book possible, Sophie Lujwain (Global Publishing and team), Cynthia McWilliams (CynCity Production Assets), My PR Team, Legible (Marketing) and those who have been champions in my life along the way, Dr. Pat

Bailey, Tyran Meredith, Sherri Shepherd, Tina Carter, Devon Johnson, Tonee Sherrill, Tanya, Ms. G & Angele.

Preface

Building the Team That Builds You

For years, I have watched capable, gifted, hardworking people wrestle with the same quiet question: *Why does progress feel so much harder than it should?* These were not people lacking talent, drive, or vision. Many were intelligent, disciplined, and deeply committed to their goals. And yet, somewhere along the journey, momentum slowed. Confidence wavered. Discouragement crept in. The temptation to quit whispered that maybe the dream was slipping further away.

I have seen this story unfold in boardrooms and classrooms, churches and coaching sessions, family conversations and private moments shared online. And I have lived it myself.

Over time, one truth became unmistakably clear: **success is never a solo act**. None of us rises without encouragement, guidance, or support from others. Whether visible or hidden, help is always part of the journey. The cultural myth of "pulling ourselves up by our bootstraps" sounds admirable, but it is incomplete. Every meaningful achievement is shaped by voices that encourage us, mentors who sharpen us, companions who stand beside us, and advocates who open doors we cannot enter alone.

This book was born from that realization.

Why This Book

I write from lived experience—my own and that of thousands of people I have encountered, mentored, worked with, taught, and served alongside over the past four decades. My path has included higher education at every level, more than twenty years in corporate America, nearly two decades as a consultant and executive coach, seven years as a college professor, and twenty-five years as a pastor and church planter. Along the way, I have raised daughters, cared for aging parents, navigated personal health challenges, built organizations, and led people through seasons of triumph and loss.

Across all of these spaces, I noticed a consistent pattern: people with similar abilities often experience very different outcomes. The difference is rarely skill alone. More often, it is support.

Some people reach the table of opportunity while others—just as capable—struggle to get close. The deciding factor is frequently the presence or absence of the right people along the way. Encouragers who breathe life into weary moments. Guides who tell the truth when growth is uncomfortable. Companions who walk through hardship without leaving. Advocates who use their influence to create access.

This book is my reflection on that reality.

The Framework: Why the 4C's Matter

The framework you will encounter throughout this book—Cheerleaders, Coaches, Comrades, and

Champions—was not developed in a classroom or research lab. It emerged from real life.

These four roles represent the essential relationships that shape both our personal and professional journeys:

- **Cheerleaders** remind us of who we are when we forget. They encourage us when we're tired, unseen, or questioning ourselves. They clap when you don't have the energy to clap for yourself. Their encouragement is like oxygen when your lungs are burning from the climb.

- **Coaches** challenge us to grow. They speak truth, refine our skills, and push us beyond comfort toward excellence. They won't let you settle for less than what they know you can achieve, and they are willing to mine out the potential that sits dormant in us.

- **Comrades** walk beside us. They share the load, sit with us in hard moments, and remind us we're not alone. In some instances, comrades can become lifelong confidants.

- **Champions** use their influence on our behalf. They open doors, speak our name in rooms we're not in, and create opportunities we couldn't access on our own.

Each role matters. No single person can—or should—be all four, and the extremely rare ones who are should be kept for a lifetime. Most of us, upon reflection, discover that gaps in our support system often explain stalled progress more than lack of ability ever could.

Some of the most pivotal moments in my own journey happened because a Champion chose to say, "Andrea should be here." Those moments changed the trajectory of my life—and they clarified why this framework matters.

What This Book Is (and Isn't)

This is not a book about networking for advantage or using people transactionally. It is about building healthy, life-giving support systems—and becoming that support for others.

You will be invited to:

- Recognize the people who have already shaped your path.

- Identify where gaps may exist in your current circle.

- Learn how to steward relationships wisely.

- Understand why some people can support you and others cannot.

- Step into these roles for others with clarity, integrity, and purpose.

Most importantly, this book will help you release unnecessary disappointment, manage expectations wisely, and move forward with courage—knowing you were never meant to do this alone.

The Invitation

My hope is that as you read, you will begin to see your journey differently. That you will recognize the voices that helped carry you further than you could have gone on your own. That you will identify where new voices are needed. And that you will feel empowered to become the kind of person who helps others rise.

We are at our best when we live connected—supported, challenged, and championed by the right people around us. And when we choose to be that for others, something powerful happens: success becomes more than achievement. It becomes legacy.

Welcome to the journey of building the team that builds you.

Table of Contents

Section I
Cheerleaders

Voices Who Inspire Hope

CHAPTER 1

EVERYBODY NEEDS A CHEERLEADER

Everyone knows what a cheerleader is, right? I am not talking about the ones who are in uniform with pom poms, but the ones that run on the sidelines of our lives, who are filled with optimism. They see you, and they see the potential in you and speak to that potential in positive and affirming ways. They may not have the same potential and may not be doing much with their own lives, but they cheer you on and brag about you to whoever will listen. When we feel like we are doing nothing, when we feel like we are failing everyone in our lives, they are there to remind us that we are "boss ladies" and "baller men" and that we are more than enough. Cheerleaders come into our lives with "word" pom-poms and uplifting clichés and say things like:

"I've got you," "you know I am in your corner," "you've got this," "there is no one better," "I see you," "I see you doing your thing," "I'm proud of you," "Ok baller, shot caller!"

They can be corny, but their source and filter are one of love. They don't care if you are tired or didn't get the numbers out to your boss on time; they don't care if you are worried about whether you are ready for a big meeting. They know nothing about your insecurities, past failures, missed opportunities, or the imposter syndrome that wants to consume you daily. They are unaware of your procrastination tendencies or the guy you are competing with, whom the CEO seems to favor. They see you and believe that you are the best of the best. They don't have to be of the same political affiliation, sexual identity, economic status, or race; they just believe in you.

Cheerleaders are those amazing people who aren't threatened by your gifts, your talent, or your charisma. They don't feel small when you shine; instead, they celebrate it. They see what you bring to the table – your creativity, your heart, your effort, and they genuinely want the world to see it too. These are the ones who speak your name in rooms you've never entered, who recommend your work even when you don't ask, and who open doors for you simply because they believe you deserve to walk through them.

A real cheerleader doesn't compete with you; they complete the energy around you. They want to see you succeed, not because it benefits them, but because your success brings them joy. They'll repost your content, share your business with their network, and tell others, "You should meet this person, they're really talented!" They talk about your skills and character when you're not around, and often, you won't even know how many times your name has come up because of them.

What's even more beautiful is that cheerleaders don't need recognition for what they do. They don't need a thank-you post or a public shoutout. They cheer because it's in their nature; they're encouragers, connectors, and supporters. They understand that someone else's light doesn't dim theirs. In fact, they know that when we all shine, the world gets brighter.

If you have cheerleaders in your life, treasure them. They're rare. They might not always be loud about it, but their quiet support makes a huge difference. They're the people who recommend you for a job, mention your name to a client, or remind others of your strengths when you're not around to do it yourself. Sometimes, they see opportunities before you do and help you step into them.

And if you're not sure you have one, be one. Be the person who talks positively about others, who lifts people up instead of tearing them down. Share someone's work, compliment their efforts, and celebrate their growth. The more we practice being cheerleaders for one another, the stronger our communities become.

So yes, cheerleaders aren't intimidated by your success. They're inspired by it. They root for you; they celebrate you, and they make sure others get to experience your brilliance, too.

Cheering Through Challenging Seasons

Cheerleaders matter most in seasons of doubt. When failure feels imminent, and confidence is running low, they are the ones who refuse to let us look down for too long. They are still clapping when time is almost gone, still believing when the odds say otherwise. And when the outcome isn't what we hoped for, they are the ones who remind us that tomorrow is a new day and another opportunity will come.

I once saw an Instagram clip of a basketball game that captured this perfectly. With seconds left on the clock, a player passed the ball to a teammate, anticipating the game-winning shot. As the ball went up, he celebrated early, believing in his teammate completely. But the shot bounced off the rim. The buzzer sounded. Game over. The player who missed the shot walked off the court with his head hanging low, defeated. Immediately, the teammate who had been cheering in anticipation of a made shot ran over, gently lifted his chin, and wrapped an arm around him as they walked off together. He never said a word, but his actions spoke clearly: You are still valuable. This moment does not define you. I am still with you.

That is the quiet power of a cheerleader.

Cheerleaders remind us that one loss does not cancel a calling, and one setback does not erase potential. They help us keep going when quitting feels reasonable. Their loyalty is not dependent on your win streak, your title, or your latest success. When we can no longer see the finish line, their consistency becomes something we can lean on.

Cheerleaders bring energy, belief, and vision into our lives. Sometimes their confidence in us is contagious. They see us winning before we've even entered the game. They hold a picture of who we can become when our own vision has grown blurry. And in moments when doubt threatens to silence us, they stand close enough to remind us that we are not alone.

Everyone wants to be cheered on. It is human nature to want to be seen, valued, and believed in—especially during the climb. Cheerleaders don't need to understand every detail of what we do or know exactly where we're headed. Their gift is simpler and more powerful than that: they choose to believe, and they stay.

CHAPTER 2

WHO CAN BE A CHEERLEADER?

Everyone can be a cheerleader, but the ones who truly make a difference are those who love deeply and care genuinely about others. A true cheerleader doesn't just say kind words; they feel them. They see the potential in people and believe in them even when the person themselves cannot. Their encouragement comes from the heart, not from duty or appearance. They become a steady voice of hope when the noise of doubt is loud. A real one is not always in the spotlight. Sometimes, they work quietly in the background, helping others rise. They may be a teacher, a parent, a mentor, or a friend. What sets them apart is their ability to see strength in others and to remind them of it. They don't need recognition or applause; their reward is in seeing someone else succeed, smile again, or rediscover their confidence. Their compassion builds people up from the inside out.

Often, cheerleaders are not the loudest people. They don't always seek recognition. What matters more is their consistency. They are there over time, even when no one is cheering back. They believe in others enough to provide encouragement, feedback, or simply presence. Sometimes it's giving advice. Other times it's being a mirror reflecting back your worth when you cannot see it yourself.

Cheerleaders can be professionals: mentors, counsellors, community leaders. For example, people who volunteer with youth mentoring programs. They help young people set goals, think through their challenges, and believe in themselves even when others doubt them. Sometimes they are activists, speaking up for justice or equality. Their voice adds strength to causes that matter, and their presence gives courage to people who are often overlooked.

More importantly, cheerleaders are everyday people: parents who believe in their child's dream, siblings who push one another to grow, friends who offer honest encouragement. Even someone who shares their own struggle can become a cheerleader because their struggle becomes proof that growth is possible. A good cheerleader understands that encouragement must be grounded in truth. They don't make false promises. They help push realistic goals, share small wins, and cheer progress. When failures happen, as they often do, they help a person get back up, learn, and try again. They don't abandon you when things are hard. They believe that people have more inside them than they might currently see. This belief shows up as patience, persistence, and faith. And that belief, repeated over time, can shift how someone sees themselves, what they try for, and how they move forward.

To become a true cheerleader in life, you don't need a stage, applause, or recognition; you need heart, patience, and purpose. The first quality you must build is focus. A cheerleader pays attention to others, not just their successes, but their struggles too. They see when someone is losing hope and step in with encouragement, reminding them that they are capable of more than they think. When it comes to hard work, supporting others isn't always easy. It takes time, effort, and genuine care. They put in the emotional work to understand, listen, and help others rise again. They don't just cheer when things are easy; they stay when things are hard. Healthy cheerleaders are determined not only to reach their own goals but also to help others reach theirs. They keep pushing forward, even when it's uncomfortable. Their determination inspires others to keep going too.

When a Community Becomes a Cheerleader

Cheerleaders aren't always individuals. Sometimes, they are communities. A city, a town, a church, or even a neighborhood can become a collective voice of encouragement that shapes confidence, courage, and identity. When people feel celebrated where they live, worship, and serve, something powerful happens—they begin to believe that their dreams are possible right where they are.

Healthy communities cheer by creating environments where people feel seen and supported. They celebrate effort, not just outcomes or perceived success. They honor growth, not just achievement. When a city celebrates its artists, entrepreneurs, educators, caregivers, and leaders, it sends a message: You matter here. When a town shows up for its young people, its elders, and its vulnerable, it becomes a place where hope has room to grow. In fact, there is nothing like a citywide parade in a small town when someone does well and the whole town comes out to cheer!

Churches, in particular, have a unique opportunity to serve as cheerleaders for the people they shepherd. At their best, churches are not performance stages; they are safe spaces. They are places where people can show up imperfect, weary, or unsure and still be met with encouragement and belief. A church that cheers well reminds people that their worth isn't tied to their productivity, their past, or their platform. It calls out purpose before success and faith before certainty. If you have ever watched an award show, you most likely have heard, 'I started playing the drums or piano at church when I was a kid.' For decades, the church has been a place for young people to learn, grow, and make mistakes while being cheered on by supportive congregants.

A cheering community doesn't compete with its own people—it champions them. It doesn't hoard opportunity—it shares it. It doesn't silence new voices—it amplifies them. Whether through mentorship programs, small groups, local initiatives, or simply consistent affirmation, communities that cheer help people rise with confidence rather than fear.

I've seen what happens when communities get this right. People take risks they would have never taken alone. Leaders emerge who never saw themselves as leaders. Dreams that once felt unrealistic begin to feel reachable. Encouragement becomes contagious. Hope becomes infectious.

But being a cheering community is intentional work. It requires listening. It requires inclusion (a controversial word in our society today). It requires celebrating progress even when the outcome is still unfolding. It means clapping for people before and during the win, not just after it.

Imagine what could change if our cities cheered for possibility instead of perfection. If our churches spoke life instead of pressure. If our neighborhoods believed in each other out loud. When a community becomes a cheerleader, it doesn't just support individuals—it transforms culture.

And perhaps the most beautiful part is this: communities that cheer don't just change lives—they create legacies. Long after programs end and leaders move on, people remember how a place made them feel. They remember who believed in them. They remember where they were first cheered on.

Managing Expectations

Most of us expect our families to be our loudest, most loyal cheerleaders. If life were simple, that expectation would make perfect sense—and the disappointment wouldn't cut as deeply when it isn't met. But the truth is, the dream you carry belongs to you. The vision you've been given for your life may not be as clear—or as compelling—to those who love you most.

Family members often see us through familiar lenses: childhood mistakes, past missteps, or ideas we once shared that never materialized. They may struggle to separate who we were from who we are becoming. Add to that sibling rivalry, unspoken comparisons, generational limitations, or even unhealed insecurities, and suddenly support feels complicated. Sometimes, without intending to, people resist cheering because your progress highlights places where they feel stuck.

I experienced this early in life. Growing up, my sisters and I had access to opportunities that many of our extended family did not. We traveled, attended private schools, and lived differently. Instead of being celebrated, we were labeled "bougie," as if wanting more from life meant believing we were better than others. That narrative was never true, but it revealed something deeper: for some, ambition felt like arrogance because it challenged the limits they had accepted for themselves. As a result, milestones like college acceptance, business ventures, or corporate success weren't celebrated—they were quietly resented.

Sometimes the deepest disappointment comes from parents who can only see success through the framework of their own experience. I once spoke with a friend who worked as an engineer in aerospace during the 1980s. In his industry, advancement required moving between companies—each move bringing growth and increased compensation. But his parents had spent their entire careers in one place, believing loyalty meant staying put. When he shared news of promotions and raises, they couldn't celebrate. Not because they weren't proud, but because they couldn't understand a path so different from their own. Their silence wasn't rejection—it was limitation.

And sometimes it's friends. The ones you grew up with. The ones you expected to celebrate your wins instinctively. When they don't, the confusion can be just as painful as the hurt. Often, it's not jealousy—it's fear. Fear that your growth means distance. Fear that your next chapter won't include them. Fear that your success forces them to confront their own unrealized potential. Even when unintentional, that fear can silence encouragement.

This is not to say that family and friends can't be cheerleaders—many are. But unmet expectations must not become obstacles. When you repeatedly explain your vision, justify your effort, or minimize your progress to make others comfortable, it's time for an internal decision. You must choose to keep moving, with or without applause.

The absence of cheers does not invalidate your calling. Sometimes the fruit of your perseverance becomes the proof others need. Sometimes it doesn't. Either way, your responsibility remains the same: to honor the vision you were given and keep pressing forward.

Cheering for a Cause

Not all cheerleaders are cheering for a single person. Some are called to cheer for something bigger than themselves—a cause, a community, a truth that needs a voice. These cheerleaders don't just offer encouragement; they create momentum. They speak when silence feels safer. They stand when others hesitate. And their courage becomes an invitation for others to believe that change is possible.

Cheering for a cause requires a different kind of strength. It often means standing alone before standing together. It means enduring criticism, misunderstanding, and resistance—sometimes from the very people you hoped would support you. But true cause-driven cheerleaders are not motivated by applause or affirmation. They are moved by conviction. Something inside them knows, this matters, and that inner clarity fuels them even when the response is uncertain.

Consider Greta Thunberg. As a teenager, she stepped forward to advocate for environmental responsibility at a global level. She faced skepticism, mockery, and dismissal—often because of her age. It would have been easy to retreat, to return to a quieter, more conventional path. Instead, she chose to cheer louder. Her voice, once solitary, sparked a movement. In doing so, she showed an entire generation that courage isn't the absence of fear—it's the decision to speak anyway. Her willingness to stand for what she believed in reminded others that waiting for the perfect moment is often the enemy of meaningful action.

History is filled with cheerleaders for causes whose voices reshaped the world. Dr. Martin Luther King Jr. is one such example. We often celebrate his speeches, marches, and leadership, but we sometimes forget the cost. Cheering for justice and equality made him a household name—but it also placed his life in constant danger and ultimately cost him everything. His encouragement of the disenfranchised was not performative; it was sacrificial. His voice carried hope, but it also carried consequence.

What makes a cheerleader for a cause so powerful is not volume—it's motivation. They are not driven by recognition, but by responsibility. Whether loud or quiet, their encouragement flows from an internal alignment that says, this is worth standing for. Their energy reignites belief in people who have grown tired of hoping. Their courage gives others permission to act.

When someone cheers with conviction and compassion, it creates a chain reaction. One voice emboldens another. One act of courage invites many more. Soon, what began as a solitary stand becomes a shared movement. Cheering for a cause reminds us that encouragement is not always about comfort—it is often about calling. And when done with integrity, it has the power to awaken purpose far beyond the individual.

CHAPTER 3

WHEN THERE ARE NO CHEERLEADERS TO CHEER

There will be seasons when no one is cheering. No applause. No encouragement. No visible support. Just silence. And silence has a way of making you question yourself—your ability, your calling, even whether the effort is worth it. Cheerleaders often help affirm and validate us, so when they are absent, doubt can creep in quickly.

These are the moments when you must learn how to become your own cheerleader.

You won't always have a crowd. You won't always have affirmation. And if forward progress depends on applause, momentum will stall the moment the noise fades. There will be seasons when no one sees the discipline, the sacrifice, the loneliness, or the work happening behind the scenes. But it is often in those quiet stretches that character is forged and integrity is revealed. This is where confidence matures—when you learn to believe in what has been placed inside you even without external validation. Remember when inspiration runs out and motivation is low; that is when discipline steps forward and urges us on and reminds us to cheer for ourselves.

One of the dangers of success is learning to live *between the claps*. When affirmation becomes the fuel, silence becomes the threat. The real question then becomes: do you trust the work you've put in enough to keep going when no one is watching? Do you believe in your preparation, your calling, and God's plan for your life strongly enough to move forward without an "attaboy" or an "attagirl"?

I was reminded of this during the NBA season played inside the bubble during the pandemic. Players who were used to performing before tens of thousands of fans suddenly had none. No roar of the crowd. No boos from opposing teams. Just quiet gyms and echoing footsteps. The league even tried to recreate the feeling of fans— virtual screens, recorded cheers—because they understood something deeply human: people perform better when they feel supported.

But eventually, players had to adjust. They had to find motivation internally. They had to compete without relying on external energy. That's what maturity looks like: learning to perform with excellence even when the atmosphere changes. I would also add that my team, the Lakers, made that adjustment and won the championship that year during Covid, and while some discounted the title, others noted how winning without cheerleaders made it even more valuable!

Coco Gauff modeled this kind of mental strength beautifully. In one match, she could hear the crowd cheering for her opponent. Instead of letting it discourage her, she made a conscious decision: I'm going to hear it as if they're cheering for me. She changed the name in her head and used the energy as fuel. That is what resilience looks like: rewriting the narrative when circumstances don't cooperate.

So, the next time you feel unseen—at work, in your family, or in a season where your efforts go unnoticed—remember this: silence does not equal insignificance. This may be your Coco Gauff moment. Flip the script in your mind. Tell yourself the truth: *They may not see it yet, but I know who I am.*

Sometimes the loudest crowd you will ever have is the one you build inside yourself. I am capable. I am prepared. I can do this.

And here's the deeper truth: the most powerful cheerleaders in life are often the ones who teach you how to cheer for yourself. They don't just celebrate your wins—they equip you to keep going when the crowd goes silent.

CHAPTER 4

CHEERLEADERS WHO INSPIRE

Cheerleaders don't always have to be people you have direct contact with. They can be people whose lives you watch from a distance and see how they cheer on others, and it inspires and encourages you.

If there is a modern example of what it looks like to be a true cheerleader, it is Oprah Winfrey. Oprah didn't just build success for herself—she built belief in others. Over the course of her career, she has used her platform to amplify voices, validate stories, and remind people that their lives and ideas matter. She has cheered for authors before the world knew their names, elevated thinkers before they had audiences, and affirmed everyday people who simply needed someone to say, *"I see you."*

What makes Oprah's encouragement so powerful is that it has never been performative. Her belief in others is intentional, consistent, and deeply human. She doesn't cheer to be seen; she cheers because she understands the transformative power of affirmation. She has said countless times that one of the greatest gifts you can give someone is the belief that they are enough and capable of more.

What many people don't realize, however, is that Oprah herself learned how to cheer from someone who cheered for *her*—the incomparable Ms. Maya Angelou. Long before Oprah became a global icon, Ms. Angelou was one of her most trusted voices. She affirmed Oprah's worth when the world tried to define her by her past. She spoke wisdom into moments of doubt. She reminded Oprah who she was when pressure, criticism, and expectation threatened to distort her sense of self.

Ms. Angelou once told Oprah, *"When you learn, teach. When you get, give."* That philosophy became a guiding principle in Oprah's life and leadership. Maya didn't just mentor Oprah; she championed her—calling out her greatness before it was fully visible, encouraging her to walk with integrity, courage, and compassion.

In many ways, Oprah became the cheerleader she once needed. She took what was poured into her and multiplied it for millions. That is the full circle of cheerleading: being seen, being encouraged, and then turning around to do the same for others. Oprah's life reminds us that cheerleaders don't just inspire hope in the moment—they create a legacy of belief that echoes far beyond themselves.

Sometimes cheerleaders are not seen as cheerleaders until others have a reason to tell their story. I think of

Kobe Bryant and all the stories that have come to the surface after he passed. NBA player after NBA player has posted stories or, while being interviewed, speaks about how Kobe had his killer instinct in his alter ego of "The Mamba" but was an outstanding cheerleader for so many other players in the league. Players spoke about how he would call them and congratulate them or reach out and encourage them in their game or, in tough times, let them know things would be ok.

I will talk more about Kobe Bryant later in the Champion Section but if you are a basketball fan, then you know Kobe was the biggest cheerleader for girls playing sports. He would show up to games, mentor girl basketball players like Sabrina Ionescu, who was a mentee of Bryant, or Diana Taurasi, affectionately calling her the "White Mamba." There were countless others, but none more important than his daughter Gigi and her AAU basketball team, which he coached. In fact, he died on the way to one of their games along with his beautiful daughter and some of her teammates and parents.

Others serve as cheerleaders through their books, talks, and podcast interviews, like Brené Brown. Her work is a powerful example of how someone can inspire others from a distance. Brené has this rare ability to speak directly to the heart. She doesn't tell you to be fearless; she invites you to be brave right in the middle of fear. Her message about courage, vulnerability, and the quiet strength that comes from owning your story has changed the way so many people see themselves and the world around them.

What I love most about Brené is that she doesn't just talk about courage, she lives it. Through her honesty, humor, and openness, she shows us that vulnerability isn't weakness; it's strength refined through truth. Listening to her feels like sitting with a trusted friend who reminds you that it's okay to be imperfect, to fall, to rise again, and to keep showing up.

Her words carry both warmth and wisdom. She doesn't just share research, she shares humanity. You feel seen and understood, and you start to believe that maybe, just maybe, you can be brave enough to show up fully as yourself. That's what a true cheerleader does: they help you find your own courage.

Brené's work reminds us that bravery doesn't mean being fearless; it means moving forward even when fear walks beside you. Her grounded research, drawn from real stories and lived experiences, gives her message a depth that's rare. I admire her dedication—the hours she must have spent listening, coding, and reflecting on thousands of voices, all to reveal the patterns of our shared humanity.

What I've learned from her is that courage grows through connection. Her writing teaches us to live wholeheartedly to be kinder, more compassionate, and more authentic, both with ourselves and with others. Brené Brown is the kind of cheerleader who might never meet you but somehow still makes you braver. May her work continue to open hearts, deepen authenticity, and remind us all that we are worthy, we belong, and we are enough exactly as we are.

When Cheering Comes at a Cost

There are times when choosing to cheer for the disenfranchised will cause you to be misunderstood. Cheering for others is not always safe, and even the purest intentions can be misinterpreted. Advocacy can be inconvenient to systems that benefit from silence, and encouragement for justice is often reframed as disruption.

Colin Kaepernick's story illustrates this reality clearly. His decision to kneel during the national anthem was an act of conscience—an effort to draw attention to racial injustice and police violence against people of color. Yet his stance was widely misread as divisive and unpatriotic, particularly by those invested in preserving the status quo. The result was costly. He was ostracized from the NFL, not because of his performance, but because of his principles.

What moves me most about Colin Kaepernick is not simply his courage, but his clarity. He did not waver in explaining his position, even when the personal cost became clear. As he stated plainly, he could not show pride in symbols that, in his view, represented ongoing oppression. For him, the issue was larger than football. It was about human dignity, accountability, and justice.

His example reminds us that being a cheerleader does not always look like celebration. Sometimes it looks like a sacrifice. Sometimes it means standing—or kneeling—alone. When you choose to cheer for what matters, you may lose applause, access, or comfort. But what you gain is integrity. And integrity has a way of outlasting public opinion.

What began as one quiet, personal act of conviction grew into a global conversation. His protest gave voice to those who had felt unseen and unheard, and it helped raise awareness of systemic inequities far beyond the world of sports. In doing so, he demonstrated that real leadership often begins without permission and continues without guarantees.

True cheerleaders are not always smiling. Sometimes they are steady. Sometimes they are resolute. They challenge systems, disrupt complacency, and risk misunderstanding so others can live with greater freedom. Today, the impact of Kaepernick's stand can be seen in countless individuals who now speak up, organize, advocate, and work toward a more just world. His example reminds us that courage is not the absence of fear—it is the decision to act in spite of it.

One person's conviction can awaken the conscience of many. And when that happens, cheering becomes more than encouragement—it becomes change.

Cheering Without Applause

Not all costly cheerleading happens on a public stage. In fact, some of the most courageous encouragement happens quietly, far from cameras or headlines.

I think of a manager who chose to advocate for a junior employee who was consistently overlooked because she didn't "fit the culture." She was talented, diligent, and prepared, but she didn't network well, didn't self-promote, and didn't look like what leadership had historically rewarded. Speaking up for her meant risking her reputation. It meant being labeled difficult. It meant pushing against unspoken norms that were easier to ignore than confront.

That manager knew the cost and chose to speak anyway. In meetings where it would have been safer to stay silent, they highlighted her contributions. When others dismissed her potential, they challenged the narrative. When promotions were discussed, they insisted her name be considered. The result was uncomfortable. Relationships shifted. Opportunities narrowed for the advocate. But the employee was eventually promoted—and more importantly, she was seen.

That is cheerleading with conviction. No applause followed. No recognition came. But the impact was real. A life changed. The ceiling cracked. A precedent set.

This kind of cheerleader understands that encouragement is not always loud or celebrated. Sometimes it is steady, persistent, and costly. It means choosing justice over comfort, advocacy over approval, and integrity over ease. These are the cheerleaders who remind us that courage doesn't always come with affirmation—it often comes with resistance.

Cheerleaders help us believe that something is possible. They lift our heads when we're discouraged, remind us of our worth, and speak hope when doubt is loud. But belief, while powerful, is only the beginning. Once we're on our feet and moving forward, we need more than applause—we need direction; we need wisdom. That's where coaches come in. Cheerleaders restore our confidence; coaches help us translate that confidence into growth. Encouragement ignites the journey, but coaching teaches us how to walk it well.

Section II
Coaches

The Strategy Behind the Spirit

CHAPTER 5

MAXIMIZING YOUR POTENTIAL

"A coach is someone who tells you what you don't want to hear, who has you see what you don't want to see, so you can be who you have always known you could be." – **Tom Landry.**

From golfers to football teams to high school speech Coaches, to C-Suite Executives, just about anyone who aspires to do anything great does so with having had a coach along the way. The opening quote encapsulates what I believe excellently. In this TikTok age we live in, a plethora of life coaches have popped up seemingly overnight, causing many to doubt the effectiveness and/or necessity of having that role in our lives. However, I submit to you that most of us get to a point in life where the effectiveness of our ability to reach the pinnacle of our influence and gifting on our own runs out. Coaches can see the greatness in us like the cheerleaders, but they also possess the ability to pull that greatness out of us and help us course correct when necessary. From Venus and Serena Williams to Tiger, Tom Brady, Meryl Streep, and Viola Davis, all of them have utilized coaches to help them reach levels of greatness that were always in them but needed mining by someone who had enough insight to speak to it and skillfully and with inspiration draw it out of them.

How might coaching fit in your arena of life? I am so glad you asked! Many of the women who are reading this are managers and have hit the proverbial glass ceiling, and perhaps you need a coach's voice to collaborate with you on what moves to make and when, or how to negotiate your salary so that it doesn't fall in the national average of 83 cents on the dollar compared to men for the same position. Perhaps a coach can help you realize you can go for that job opening that you are intimidated to apply for, or tell you off the ledge when you are overwhelmed by the things that are encroaching on your life.

The Power of Coaches

Coaches play a critical role in the workplace—especially when pressure is high, progress feels stalled, and leadership dynamics become challenging. For many men, a coach provides something rare: a safe, judgment-free space to process frustration, regulate emotions, and gain perspective when work environments feel overwhelming.

Contrary to the outdated narrative that men don't feel, men often carry emotions deeply—but are given few healthy outlets to express them. A coach creates room to explore fear, doubt, anger, and anxiety without shame. This emotional clarity is not a weakness; it is a strategic advantage. When emotions are acknowledged and filtered constructively, decision-making improves, communication sharpens, and confidence stabilizes.

Coaches also help uncover blind spots—those areas we all have but rarely see on our own. When men feel stuck or unsure why advancement has slowed, a coach can identify patterns, behaviors, or skill gaps that may be limiting growth. Because coaching relationships are built on trust and confidentiality, they allow for honest reflection without fear of judgment. That honesty becomes the foundation for meaningful progress.

Coaches See What We Can't—or Won't

Anyone who has worked with a fitness coach understands this principle well. A good coach somehow knows you can do more—one more rep, one more lap, one more push—when you are convinced your tank is empty. Their belief often precedes your own.

I experienced this firsthand when I committed to being "Fit by Fifty." I had already been working out consistently, but once I hired a coach, everything changed. They pushed me beyond what I thought was possible—not recklessly, but intentionally. Even when I insisted I had nothing left, they saw capacity I hadn't yet accessed. That's the power of coaching: seeing potential clearly when the client's vision is clouded by fatigue, doubt, or fear.

Great coaches don't just address physical limits; they confront mental and emotional barriers. They help dismantle the internal narratives that keep us stuck and replace them with truth, discipline, and forward momentum.

Why Coaches Matter

Coaches help us regulate emotions, sharpen focus, confront blind spots, and stay accountable to the future we say we want. They see what we overlook, challenge what holds us back, and believe in what's possible—sometimes before we do.

Growth rarely happens in isolation. And when pressure rises, a coach becomes not just a guide, but a stabilizing force—helping us move forward with clarity, courage, and confidence.

One of the greatest gifts a coach offers is accountability. It's easy to let yourself off the hook. It's much harder when someone is expecting you to show up—fully, consistently, and honestly.

Coaches hold you accountable to the goals you say you want to achieve. They challenge excuses, call out patterns, and keep you focused when motivation fades. They don't just see the mountaintop; they help you identify the steps required to reach it.

As a coach, I work with women who want to become the best version of themselves—financially, emotionally, physically, mentally, and relationally. Often, people excel in one or two areas while other parts of their lives lack structure or discipline. My role is to help bring alignment, to push clients beyond comfort, and to help them see that what they desire is not only possible—it's attainable with intentional effort.

Coaches are especially valuable after failure. When a goal isn't met, or momentum is lost, self-doubt can creep in quickly. A coach is not emotionally attached to the failure the way we are. They are not jaded by it. They don't carry the same fear or hesitation. Instead, they lend confidence, perspective, and encouragement—reminding us that one setback does not negate our ability to succeed.

Trust Is Not Optional

Trust is the foundation of every effective coaching relationship. Without it, coaching becomes transactional instead of transformational. When trust is absent, even well-intentioned guidance can be questioned, resisted, or ignored. A coach may ask you to try something unfamiliar or uncomfortable, but without trust, doubt creeps in—and progress stalls.

Trust creates openness. It allows you to receive feedback without becoming defensive and gives you the courage to experiment with new approaches, even when they stretch you beyond your comfort zone. It makes room for vulnerability—for admitting when something isn't working and being honest about why. While a coach can offer insight and strategy, meaningful growth only happens when you are willing to let them see the full picture.

That kind of trust doesn't happen overnight. It's built through consistency, respect, and clear communication. A trustworthy coach listens well, honors confidentiality, and follows through on their commitments. They create an environment where honesty is met with support, not judgment. In return, the client shows up willing to do the work—ready to be truthful, receptive, and engaged in the process.

When trust flows both ways, momentum increases. Growth deepens. Confidence strengthens. Coaching becomes a partnership rather than a performance. That is why trust is not optional—it is the ground on which everything else is built.

Mentors vs. Coaches

Mentors and coaches serve different—but equally valuable—roles. Understanding the distinction can save you time, money, and unnecessary frustration.

Mentors are often people who are already doing what you aspire to do. They are out ahead of you on the path and can offer perspective based on lived experience. Mentors show you what's possible by example. They share how they navigated challenges, avoided pitfalls, and made key decisions along the way. Their wisdom comes from having *been there*. Because of this, mentorship often unfolds over a long period of time and may even last a lifetime. Mentors don't always give step-by-step instructions; instead, they model principles, habits, and leadership. Their influence is often quiet but profound.

Sometimes mentors aren't people you know personally. They may be public figures whose books, interviews, podcasts, or newsletters offer insight and guidance. While this type of mentorship isn't relational in the traditional sense, it can still be powerful—especially when you don't yet have access to someone in your immediate circle who has walked the road you're trying to travel.

Coaches, on the other hand, are active partners in your growth. Coaching is typically structured, intentional, and time-bound. A coach meets with you consistently, listens closely, challenges your thinking, helps regulate emotions, and holds you accountable to the goals you say you want to achieve. While mentors lead primarily by example, coaches lead through engagement, feedback, and strategy.

A coach doesn't have to be ahead of you in the same way a mentor often is—but they must be skilled in helping you move forward. Coaching focuses less on how they did it and more on how you will do it.

How to Know What You Need

Before searching, ask yourself a simple question: Am I looking for wisdom from someone who has walked this road—or support from someone who will help me navigate it right now?

If you need perspective, inspiration, and long-term guidance, a mentor may be what you're seeking. If you need clarity, accountability, and forward momentum, a coach is likely the better fit. Finding the right coach takes time and patience. There is no one-size-fits-all approach. Every coach has a different style, and every client has unique goals and needs. It's normal—and wise—to speak with a few coaches before choosing one.

A good coach should make you feel both supported and stretched. They should challenge you without shaming you and create a space where honesty, vulnerability, and growth are possible. Alignment matters. If the connection isn't there, progress will be limited.

Referrals are often the best place to start. Ask trusted friends, mentors, or colleagues if they've worked with a coach they respect. Personal recommendations carry weight because they come from lived experience. Don't hesitate to ask potential coaches about their approach, experience, successes, and even the kinds of clients they work with best.

A Word on Integrity in Coaching

A good coach will be honest about whether they are the right fit for you. Coaching is not about convincing someone to sign on—it's about stewarding responsibility well.

I've had prospective clients whose goals fell outside my area of expertise. In those cases, I chose honesty over income. Accepting an assignment I couldn't serve well would have wasted their time, money, and trust—and compromised my integrity. A coach who promises everything is often the one least prepared to deliver.

The right coaching relationship feels like a partnership. You feel seen, heard, and respected. Growth is challenging, but it doesn't feel manipulative or forced. When that alignment exists, coaching becomes a powerful catalyst—not just for performance, but for personal transformation.

CHAPTER 6

HOW TO PICK THE RIGHT COACH FOR YOU?

Picking the right coach can take a bit of time; there's no "one size fits all". Often, you have to interview a few before you find one that aligns with your goals, that you feel will motivate you and challenge you to be the best version of yourself, and one that you'll feel safe enough with to be honest and vulnerable. One of the best ways to get started is to ask for referrals from friends or coworkers who have used coaches before. Personal references are always a good thing because you will be able to talk to someone who has a history with that coach.

The coach also has to feel like they are able to help you accomplish your goals, and a good coach will be honest enough to say whether or not they believe that they are a good fit for you or that they can help you achieve your goals. the coaches who are in it for just a money play will tell you anything and try to convince you that they can do everything when in fact sometimes personalities don't mesh. I have had clients who, after we had the initial interview and I understood what their goals were and what they were trying to accomplish, I realized that I didn't have the expertise to help them get to where they wanted to go. To have taken that assignment would have not only frustrated them, wasted their money, and potentially set me up for a bad review or reputation, and none of that is worth it.

When people ask me how to choose the right coach, I always smile, because I've been there. I remember sitting at my desk years ago, staring at a list of names, wondering, "How do I know which one is right for me?" Back then, I thought I needed someone who understood my exact industry, who had walked my same road. What I've learned over time is that finding the right coach has less to do with what's on their résumé but more so with whether they make you feel like you can maximize the gifts and potential you possess and if they have the skill to mine greatness out of you.

Life moves fast. Most of us are busy trying to outperform yesterday's version of ourselves, chasing the next milestone before we've even celebrated the last one. Coaching gives you something precious in the middle of all that noisy space. It's a pause, a moment to breathe, to think, to ask yourself, "What really matters right now?" The right coach helps you see your blind spots and your brilliance at the same time. They don't give you answers, they help you find your own.

When I started working with my first coach, I thought I needed someone who could help me be more productive, more efficient, more everything. But that wasn't what I needed at all. What I really needed was someone who could hold space for me to think. She didn't talk about strategy or spreadsheets; she asked questions that pulled me back to my core values, the parts of myself I had buried under ambition. That's when I understood that coaching isn't about adding more to your life; it's about clearing space for what truly belongs there.

A lot of people tell me, "I'll look for a coach once I know exactly what I want." I always say, "Don't wait." You don't have to have everything figured out before you begin. Sometimes, not knowing is the perfect place to start. Some of my biggest breakthroughs came when I walked into a coaching session and simply said, "I don't know." There's something powerful about admitting that. It opens the door for discovery.

Myths About Coaching

There's the myth that coaching is only for people who are struggling. That couldn't be further from the truth. Some of the most accomplished, grounded people I know have coaches. They're not broken; they're intentional. Coaching keeps you aligned with your growth instead of drifting through it. It's not about fixing what's wrong; it's about amplifying what's right.

Another thing people often say is, "I don't have time for coaching." I used to believe that, too. Until one day, my own coach looked at me and said, "If you can't find an hour for yourself, what are you really working so hard for?" That question stopped me cold. I realized I had built a life so full of doing that I had forgotten how to simply be. Now I protect that hour fiercely. It's my weekly reset button, a space to think, reflect, and recharge.

So how do you know if a coach is right for you? The answer is a simple connection. You should feel it in your gut. In that very first conversation, pay attention not to what they say, but how you feel when you talk to them. Do you feel safe? Do you feel understood? Do you feel gently challenged, like you're being called to step into your best self? If you walk away from that first meeting feeling lighter, more curious, or just a little more awake, that's a good sign. Coaching works best when there's trust, when you know this is someone who will celebrate your wins and hold you accountable with love, not judgment.

When I meet a potential coach, I don't look for perfection. I listen for presence. Are they truly listening to me, or are they just waiting for their turn to speak? Do they make me feel like a project to be fixed or a person to be understood? The best coaches don't perform; they hold space. Their power is in their attention, the kind that makes you realize you've been skimming the surface of your own life and now, finally, you're ready to go deeper.

One thing I've learned over the years is that the right coach will always make you braver. They won't let you hide behind excuses. They'll remind you that you are capable of more than you think, but they'll also honor the pace that's right for you. They won't rush your growth; they'll walk beside you as you grow into it.

And trust me, chemistry matters. You can have a coach with all the credentials in the world, but if you don't click with them, it won't work. Coaching is a relationship built on honesty. If you can't be completely yourself, messy, confused, hopeful, and real, then you haven't found your person yet. Keep looking. When it's right, you'll feel it.

At the heart of it all, choosing the right coach is about trusting yourself. Listen to your intuition. Your body knows before your brain does. If you leave a session feeling seen, inspired, and grounded, you're in the right place. If you walk away feeling small, unheard, or confused, that's not your coach, and that's okay. The right one will meet you where you are and help you grow from there.

I tell people all the time, coaching isn't about fixing your life; it's about learning to live it more fully. A great coach doesn't hand you a plan. They hand you a mirror. And when you investigate it, you don't just see who you are; you start to see who you're becoming.

So, if you're thinking about getting a coach, don't overthink it. You don't need the perfect words or the perfect moment. You just need to start. Reach out. Have the conversation. See what happens. The right coach won't change who you are; they'll help you remember.

One final thought when it comes to choosing the right coach: always remember that expertise in many cases does matter. It's not just about finding someone with a fancy title or a long list of clients; it's about finding someone who truly understands the terrain you're trying to navigate. Ideally, your coach should have a real-world connection to your goals. That doesn't mean they must have held the exact position you're aspiring to, but they should possess a proven record of achievement, discipline, and awareness of what it takes to thrive in challenging environments.

For example, if your goal is to move into a senior leadership role, your coach doesn't necessarily need to have been a vice president or CEO. However, they should be someone who has experienced professional growth, handled workplace challenges, and understands corporate dynamics, such as internal politics, competition for advancement, and how to build influence with integrity. A coach who has walked through their own version of success will recognize the unspoken pressures and subtle shifts that happen as you climb higher.

Think of it this way: you wouldn't hire a financial advisor who can't manage their own finances. If someone hasn't demonstrated the ability to create stability and success in their own life, it's unlikely they can guide you toward yours. The same principle applies to coaching. The best coaches lead not just from theory, but from experience and authenticity.

And although I said that was my final thought, here's one more worth holding on to: don't take criticism from people you wouldn't take advice from. Everyone has an opinion, but not every opinion is worth your energy. Choose carefully whose voices you allow to shape your path. Seek guidance from those who've proven they can turn challenges into growth and who genuinely want to see you succeed. Surround yourself with mentors, not mere critics.

CHAPTER 7

A NEW COACH FOR A NEW LEVEL

There are seasons when a coach has taken you as far as they can—and seasons when you have taken yourself as far as you can. Growth eventually requires a shift. What worked to get you here may not be what will take you forward.

At higher levels, progress demands perspective. It becomes essential to choose a coach who can see the *next* version of you and has the skill to help you get there. I often tell my clients not to hire a financial coach who is not financially stable or practicing the principles they teach. While a coach does not have to stand on the highest rung themselves, they must be technically sound, emotionally intelligent, and proven in guiding others upward.

Nearly every high-performing athlete, CEO, or creative you admire has relied on coaching at pivotal moments. Talent alone eventually plateaus. Discipline needs direction. Growth needs structure. The people who go the farthest are rarely the most gifted—they are the most teachable. Coaching is not a sign of weakness; it is a sign of wisdom.

The right coach doesn't just help you win; they help you become someone who can *handle* the win. They refine your thinking, sharpen your focus, and strengthen your inner life so success doesn't outpace your character.

One of the clearest examples of this is Dr. Bill Campbell, often called *"The Coach of Silicon Valley."* What makes his story remarkable is that he wasn't a tech expert at all. He began his career as a football coach, yet he became a trusted advisor to leaders like Steve Jobs, Eric Schmidt, and Jeff Bezos.

Bill's gift wasn't technical mastery—it was human insight. He saw the person behind the title. He asked leaders not only about performance, but also about relationships, integrity, and emotional health. When Steve Jobs was fired from Apple, Bill didn't see failure; he saw unrefined potential. He coached Steve through that difficult season, helping him mature as a leader and human being. When Steve returned to Apple, he didn't just build products—he built trust, culture, and vision. Bill's coaching reminds us that the right coach doesn't just elevate performance; they transform the leader.

Athletes understand this instinctively. Tiger Woods is a powerful example. Even at the top of his game, Tiger chose to rebuild his swing and work with new coaches. That decision required humility—the willingness to be taught when the world already considered him a master. His coaches didn't just adjust mechanics; they helped him refine focus, mindset, and resilience. Tiger's longevity is proof that greatness is not sustained by talent alone, but by a commitment to continual learning.

And that's the truth about coaching: it's not about being told what to do; it's about being guided toward who you can become. When I look at the lives of people like Bill Campbell, Tiger Woods, Steve Jobs, and others, I see a common thread: they all embraced growth through guidance. None of them were too proud to be taught, too comfortable to change, or too successful to listen.

Each of their stories teaches a powerful truth: the right coach doesn't just help you reach your goals; they help you reach your potential. They see in you what you sometimes can't see in yourself. I believe we all need that kind of person in our lives, someone who helps us stretch, improve, and believe again. A coach doesn't just train your hands; they shape your heart. They help you move from where you are to where you're meant to be. Because at every new level of your life, a new kind of coach will be waiting, ready to guide, challenge, and help you grow into the best version of yourself.

There are so many more examples, but a thread that runs through them all is that they never stopped being a student. Even when they reach what others perceive to be the pinnacle of their career, they keep learning; they remain open to being taught. They always believed there was another gear in them, another level, another opportunity to leave a powerful legacy of greatness on the earth.

A New Form of Coaching

This may feel a little controversial, but there is a new form of coaching many of us are overlooking: artificial intelligence. Every day, new AI-powered tools are emerging—tools that can help analyze data, streamline systems, generate strategy, automate repetitive tasks, and even create digital versions of your voice and workflow. Used wisely, AI can function as a powerful support system that helps leaders move faster, think more broadly, and operate with greater efficiency.

For many professionals, AI is becoming an on-demand assistant—one that never gets tired, can process massive amounts of information in seconds, and offers insight across industries. Whether you're building a business, leading a team, creating content, or managing complex decisions, AI can help you clarify ideas, explore options, and identify blind spots you may not have recognized on your own. In that sense, it can act like a strategic coach— asking questions, offering frameworks, and helping you refine your thinking.

It's understandable that this technology feels intimidating. New tools often trigger fear, especially when they challenge the way we've always worked. But like any tool, AI is neutral; its impact depends entirely on how it's used. When applied ethically and intentionally, it has the potential to elevate—not replace—human skill, creativity, and leadership. AI can help sharpen strategies, improve communication, and free up time so you can focus on what matters most: relationships, vision, and purpose.

That said, AI has limits. It can analyze patterns, but it cannot feel. It can offer suggestions, but it cannot discern calling. It can support decision-making, but it cannot replace wisdom, empathy, or lived experience. AI may help you *work* smarter, but it cannot teach you how to lead with compassion, navigate grief, or make values-based decisions. Those are human responsibilities.

The most effective leaders will not choose between AI and human coaching—they will learn how to integrate both. AI can help you prepare, organize, and execute. Human coaches help you interpret, discern, and grow. One accelerates performance; the other deepens character.

When used as a supplement—not a substitute—AI becomes a powerful ally. It helps you see more clearly, move more strategically, and steward your time more wisely. In this new era, coaching is no longer confined to one voice or one method. Growth comes from knowing which tools to use, when to use them, and how to remain grounded in your humanity while leveraging innovation.

Use With Discernment

AI is a powerful tool, but it should never replace personal responsibility, human judgment, or ethical leadership. Decisions that impact people's lives, values, and well-being require discernment, empathy, and accountability—qualities no algorithm can replicate. AI should be used to *inform* decisions, not to *abdicate* them. Each of us must remain vigilant about accuracy, bias, confidentiality, and integrity, ensuring that technology supports human dignity rather than undermines it. Wisdom lies not in using every tool available, but in knowing when—and when not—to use them, always endeavoring to use the power for good!

How might this work? I am glad you asked: imagine a business owner preparing for a major presentation or strategic shift. AI can help clarify messaging, organize talking points, analyze market trends, and even rehearse potential questions. It can highlight gaps in logic or offer alternative approaches the leader hadn't considered. But when it comes time to make the final call—how to lead the team through change, how to communicate with empathy, or how to align decisions with personal values—that work remains human. In this way, AI becomes a coaching companion, not a decision-maker: sharpening the process while leaving wisdom in the hands of the leader.

Technology may help you move faster—but wisdom ensures you're moving in the right direction.

Remember, a new level often requires a new lens. The coach who helped you start may not be the one equipped to help you scale. This isn't betrayal—it's maturity. Growth honors the past while preparing for the future. True greatness never stops learning. And the courage to invite new coaching may be the very thing that ensures your success lasts.

CHAPTER 8

YOUR COACH IS NOT YOUR PARENT

A coach is not a fan. Their job isn't to babysit you, coddle you, or tell you what you want to hear. A coach isn't there to fix you either. They are there to partner with you, to bring out the best in you, sometimes by saying the hard things that others might avoid. A good coach is honest, direct, and committed to your growth, even when their words sting a little.

Coaches often see what you can't see in yourself. And because of that, they may push you harder than you expect. Sometimes, they are toughest on the people they believe in the most. I think about the movie Love and Basketball, where Sanaa Lathan plays Monica Wright, a talented but emotional basketball player. Her coach constantly corrects her, points out her mistakes, and never seems satisfied, no matter how hard she works. Monica begins to believe that her coach simply doesn't like her and wants her off the team.

But later in the film, when a key player gets injured, the coach surprises Monica by naming her the starting point guard. Confused, Monica admits she thought her coach disliked her. The coach responds, "I ride you hard because I see potential in you. I know you have what it takes." That moment changes everything for Monica and for anyone watching. That's what true coaching looks like. A good coach challenges you because they see something worth developing. They don't waste time on people who aren't willing to grow, and they don't hold back the truth just to make you feel comfortable. If they push you hard, it's because they believe you can handle it. Their goal isn't to tear you down; it's to bring out the strength that's already inside you.

Sometimes it's hard to see that when you're in the middle of being stretched. Growth never feels easy and having someone constantly correct or challenge you can be frustrating. But the best coaches don't show up to make you feel good in the moment; they show up to make you better for the long run. They see the potential in you that you may not see yet, and they're willing to walk with you until you start believing it too.

When a coach corrects you or pushes you to do something differently, it's not because they doubt you; it's because they believe you can go further than you think. They already see the version of you that's stronger, wiser, and more confident, even before you do. A good coach can look past where you are right now and focus on who you're becoming. That's why their words can sometimes feel sharp or uncomfortable. They're not meant to hurt you but to help shape you. Their correction comes from belief, not criticism.

Think about it this way: if a coach didn't care, they wouldn't take the time to correct you at all. Indifference is easy; investment takes effort. When they stop you mid-task, ask you to try again, or challenge your excuses, they're doing it because they want to see you win. They know that progress only happens when pressure is applied. And even though that pressure can feel hard in the moment, it's often what produces real strength and confidence.

So, when your coach is hard on you, don't take it personally. Take it as a compliment. It means they believe you're capable of more, and they're willing to stay beside you until you reach it. Their firmness is a sign of faith in your potential. They see something powerful in you that you might not yet recognize, and they're committed to bringing it out. That's what real love looks like in action. It's not soft or passive; it's steady and intentional. A true coach doesn't give up when things get tough; they keep showing up, guiding, and reminding you that you're stronger than you think. They see your greatness, and they won't stop until you start seeing it too.

If a coach feels like they want it more than you do, more than likely, they will stop coaching. Eventually, there's a thought or saying: you can't want it more for them than they want it for themselves.

Coaching Is a Partnership

Coaches invest their time, energy, and heart into helping you grow. But growth is never a one-sided effort—it requires partnership. A coach can provide insight, strategy, and accountability, but they cannot do the work for you. Progress only happens when both sides show up fully.

When a coach consistently shows up prepared and on time, but you don't, it quietly communicates misalignment. When assignments go unfinished, excuses multiply, or effort is inconsistent, it signals resistance to change. Over time, these patterns discourage even the most committed coach. Coaching works best when commitment is mutual.

Comparison can also undermine growth. Constantly measuring your current coach against a previous one prevents you from receiving what this coach uniquely offers. Every coach has a different style, lens, and strength. Growth requires presence, not nostalgia. Along with that, unrealistic expectations—wanting immediate results without sustained effort—can erode trust. Real transformation takes time, patience, and humility.

Respect matters just as much as effort. Honoring financial agreements, protecting intellectual property, showing up prepared, and respecting boundaries are not small details—they are signals of seriousness. A coach wants to see you win, but they also need to know that you value the process.

Behaviors That Undermine the Coaching Relationship

Growth stalls when patterns like these go unaddressed:

- Consistently arriving late or unprepared for sessions.

- Making excuses instead of completing agreed-upon work.

- Complaining about assignments or resisting the level of effort required.

- Constantly comparing your current coach to a former one.

- Blaming the coach for lack of progress while ignoring guidance.

- Expecting quick results without sustained commitment.

- Resisting feedback or taking correction personally.

- Treating sessions casually, skipping meetings, or failing to prioritize the work.

- Failing to communicate honestly about challenges or expectations.

- Paying fees late or avoiding agreed-upon financial commitments.

- Sharing coaching materials or resources without permission.

These behaviors don't reflect a lack of potential—they reflect a lack of alignment.

Why Commitment Matters

Having a coach is a privilege, not a punishment. It means someone believes in your potential enough to challenge you, correct you, and walk with you through growth that may feel uncomfortable at times. Discomfort is often the doorway to change.

A good coach will push you—but they will also stand beside you through setbacks and breakthroughs. They are not there to carry you; they are there to remind you that you can walk this path yourself. When you remain teachable, consistent, and humble, growth becomes inevitable.

A coach may guide the way, but you are the one who must take the steps. And when you do, you won't just reach new levels—you'll discover strengths, discipline, and confidence you didn't know you had.

CHAPTER 9

ENDING A COACHING RELATIONSHIP

In every coaching journey, there comes a point when you must step back and ask yourself if the relationship is still working. The goal of coaching is to grow, move forward, and achieve goals and operating at your highest potential. But just as every season in life has a beginning, a middle, and an end, a coaching relationship does too. Knowing when to close that chapter is just as important as knowing when to start it. When you have reached the goal you set when you first started, you've grown, gained confidence, and learned to apply what you were taught, continuing the same process might not serve you anymore. It's not a failure; it's a sign of success. It means the purpose of the coaching relationship has been fulfilled. The right thing to do then is to celebrate the progress, acknowledge the growth, and let it come to an end.

At other times, a coaching relationship starts to feel heavy or stagnant. The energy shifts, the motivation drops, or you don't feel motivated to show up with the same commitment. That can be a sign that it's time to reassess. Maybe your goals have changed, perhaps you are not truly ready to move forward, or maybe the coaching style that once worked no longer fits who you are becoming. Recognizing this moment requires honesty and maturity from both the coach and the client. When the relationship reaches that crossroads, the coach can't view it as rejection; it's redirection. Every coaching experience is a partnership, and sometimes partnerships evolve. The goal is always growth for both the coach and the client. Ending with gratitude, clarity, and mutual respect allows both people to walk away stronger and ready for what's next.

Readiness Matters

One of the most overlooked challenges in coaching is readiness. Some clients genuinely want change but are not yet prepared for the internal work it requires. They may desire growth while resisting accountability, avoiding difficult conversations, or clinging to familiar patterns. Vulnerability is essential to transformation—and vulnerability is uncomfortable.

There is no shame in acknowledging that you are not ready *yet*. Wisdom lies in recognizing when to continue, when to pause, and when to transition. Coaching works best when both coach and client are aligned in honesty, effort, and timing.

Ending Well Is Part of Growing Well

When a coaching relationship ends with clarity and respect, it becomes a marker of maturity—not loss. Endings handled well preserve dignity, protect momentum, and create space for future growth. Sometimes the most powerful step forward is recognizing that one chapter has done its work and trusting that another will begin when the time is right.

I've noticed that when coaching men in particular, many want to move straight to solutions, skipping over emotional awareness or personal reflection. That's where progress can stall. Coaching isn't about telling someone what to do, it's about helping them uncover what's holding them back. If a client isn't ready to face those truths, no amount of coaching can move them forward. A good coach knows when to keep guiding and when to gently step back.

Trust is another key piece in every coaching relationship. It's the foundation everything else is built on. Without trust, the process loses its power. Trust allows both the coach and the client to speak freely, share honestly, and work together without fear. But once trust is broken, progress becomes almost impossible. Sometimes, clients stop being transparent they hold back, avoid questions, or give partial answers. Other times, the coach may cross a boundary, give too much personal advice, or blur professional lines. Either way, when trust fades, the relationship starts to crumble. And while trust takes time to build, it can be lost in a single moment.

When You Are the Coach

As a coach, your first responsibility is to protect trust. That means maintaining confidentiality, honoring boundaries, and keeping the focus on the client's growth—not your own story, needs, or emotions. Coaching is not a shared confessional; it is a sacred space created for someone else's development.

When trust is compromised and cannot be repaired, the most professional response is not to push through—it is to pause and, if necessary, end the relationship with integrity. Ending well requires just as much courage as beginning with enthusiasm. Continuing a partnership that no longer serves either party does more harm than good.

Signs a Coaching Relationship Has Reached Its End

One of the most common signs that a coaching relationship may be nearing its end is a noticeable slowdown in progress. Action becomes inconsistent. Assignments are delayed. Follow-through weakens. The energy and momentum that once fueled the work begin to fade.

Sometimes this happens because motivation has shifted. Other times, it requires a deeper level of honesty: you may not be ready for the next layer of change. Real transformation demands readiness, openness, and self-awareness—and not every season of life allows for that kind of work. Pausing does not mean you've failed; it may simply mean the timing is off.

Before concluding a coaching relationship, a skilled and ethical coach will pause to evaluate—not just the client, but themselves. Good coaches ask reflective questions such as:

- Are the sessions spaced too far apart—or too close together?

- Am I following the client's pace, or pushing beyond their readiness?

- Have I adjusted my tools and strategies to match where the client is now?

- What responsibility might I hold in the current lack of progress?

A thoughtful coach does not immediately assume resistance or lack of effort. They examine the process first. But if adjustments have been made, strategies refreshed, and support offered—and momentum still does not return—it may be time to acknowledge that the relationship has fulfilled its purpose for this season.

Releasing a client is not abandonment. It is clarity. A responsible coach may recommend a different approach, a new program, or even another coach whose style better aligns with the client's current needs. Letting go does not signal failure; it honors the integrity of the work.

The Client's Responsibility: Asking the Right Questions

Just as coaches must reflect, clients also have a role in discerning when a coaching relationship should pause or conclude. Growth is a partnership, and self-awareness matters.

Before ending a coaching relationship, clients should consider asking themselves—and their coach—questions such as:

- Am I truly applying what we've discussed, or am I avoiding the work?

- Have I been honest about my resistance, fear, or lack of readiness?

- Do I need a different coaching style—or simply a break to integrate what I've learned?

- Am I expecting the coach to motivate me instead of taking responsibility for my growth?

- Have my goals changed in ways I haven't clearly communicated?

- Is this a season to pause, reflect, or transition—not quit altogether?

These questions shift the conversation from disappointment to discernment. They help clients distinguish between discomfort that leads to growth and resistance that blocks it.

When Values or Alignment Shift

Another reason a coaching relationship may need to end is misalignment. Over time, you may discover that your values, priorities, or approach to life differ significantly from your client's. Misalignment doesn't automatically disqualify the relationship—coaching should always remain judgment-free—but it does require honesty.

If that difference begins to affect your objectivity, emotional availability, or ability to fully support the client, it must be addressed. A clear, compassionate conversation is essential. You might say:

"I want to make sure you're receiving the best possible support, and I believe another coach may be better suited for where you are right now."

That is not quitting. That is stewardship. Coaching is not about ownership; it's about helping someone move forward—even if that means releasing them into another capable set of hands.

When the Coach Needs to Pause

Sometimes, the issue isn't the client—it's the coach. Coaching requires emotional presence, empathy, creativity, and energy. Without intentional care, even the best coaches can experience burnout.

If you begin to feel consistently tired, uninspired, frustrated, or disconnected during sessions, it's time to reflect honestly. Ask yourself:

- Am I still passionate about this work?

- Am I showing up at the level my clients deserve?

Ignoring those signals doesn't just affect you—it impacts your clients. Healthy coaches create healthy coaching environments. Taking a break, reducing your caseload, or seeking supervision or coaching for yourself is not a weakness; it's wisdom.

Boredom can also be a quiet warning sign. Coaching thrives on curiosity and engagement. When the work no longer challenges or energizes you, it may be time to evolve—whether that means refining your niche, pursuing new training, or working with different types of clients.

Great coaches regularly self-check. They assess not only the client's progress, but also their own energy, mindset, and motivation. That awareness keeps the work ethical, effective, and alive.

When the Work Is Complete

One of the most rewarding reasons to end a coaching relationship is completion. This is the goal every coach hopes for—the moment when a client has grown, achieved what they set out to do, and is ready to move forward independently.

Completion is not an ending; it's evidence. Coaching is not meant to create dependency—it is meant to build capacity. When a client no longer needs you, it means you have done your job well. Celebrate that moment. Reflect together on the journey, the lessons learned, and the growth achieved.

Some clients move on permanently. Others return later for a new season of development. Either way, it's a win. Coaching is seasonal. Each season has a purpose, and wisdom lies in knowing when it's time to release with grace.

When Boundaries Are Crossed

Finally, there is one clear sign that a coaching relationship should end immediately: boundary confusion.

I once hired a fitness coach to help me stay disciplined and healthy. That was the intention. But over time, our roles quietly reversed. Instead of focusing on my training, he began using our sessions to unload his personal struggles—his marriage, finances, and frustrations. Before I realized what was happening, I was doing the listening, encouraging, and emotional labor—while still paying for the session.

That was not coaching. That was misplaced dependency.

A coach who consistently centers their own needs, stories, or struggles is no longer serving the client. Boundaries are not optional; they are foundational. When they collapse, the relationship must be addressed—or ended.

Ending Well Is Part of Coaching Well

Coaching relationships are not meant to last forever. Like therapy, they exist to equip people with tools, awareness, and confidence to move forward on their own. When the relationship has reached its natural conclusion—whether through completion, misalignment, or capacity—it is healthy to say:

"We've done meaningful work together. Now it's time for your next step."

That is not loss. That is leadership.

When the right coach is matched with a willing client, growth is not just possible—it's inevitable. And when the season ends, releasing with clarity and grace honors the work you've both done.

When Your Coach Is Too Close to You

It's tempting to believe that the person who knows you best—your spouse, partner, or close family member—would make the ideal coach. After all, they see your habits, understand your history, and care deeply about your success. But closeness, while powerful in relationships, can become a liability in coaching.

Coaching requires objectivity, structure, and emotional neutrality. Marriage and family relationships, by nature, are emotional, layered, and deeply personal. When those roles overlap, boundaries blur quickly. Feedback can feel like criticism. Accountability can feel like control. And what was meant to support growth can quietly erode trust and intimacy.

In a marriage or partnership, coaching dynamics often introduce an uneven power balance. One person becomes the "corrector," while the other becomes the "project." Over time, this can create resentment. Conversations about growth spill into personal moments. Progress updates replace affection. And what should be a safe relationship begins to feel like a performance review.

Even with the best intentions, emotional history complicates the process. A spouse or family member cannot easily separate who you *are* from who you *have been*. Old arguments, unresolved disappointments, and shared wounds can distort feedback. What might sound like professional guidance from an external coach can land as judgment or disappointment when it comes from someone whose approval matters deeply.

There's also the issue of rest. Healthy relationships require spaces where you are not being evaluated, corrected, or improved. When your partner becomes your coach, the relationship can lose its softness. There is no off switch. Growth conversations follow you into the kitchen, the car, and the bedroom. That constant pressure can exhaust both people.

This doesn't mean spouses and family members shouldn't encourage, support, or celebrate each other. They absolutely should. But encouragement is different from coaching. Support says, *"I believe in you."* Coaching says, *"Here's how you need to change."* Those messages serve different purposes and require different containers.

In strong marriages and partnerships, it is often healthier for each person to have external coaches or mentors who can speak objectively, challenge without emotional charge, and hold accountability without relational risk.

This protects the intimacy of the relationship while still honoring the desire to grow.

I had a close friend whose husband happened to be a self-help coach, confident, passionate, and very successful in his work. When she decided she wanted to grow personally and hire a life coach to help her reach new goals, her husband immediately said, "Why hire someone else? I can coach you."

At first, it seemed like a good idea. After all, he was a professional. But within a few sessions, things got tense. He was harder on her than he was on his clients, constantly critiquing her efforts and pushing her beyond what was healthy. Meanwhile, she became increasingly resentful. She'd see how patient and kind he was with his clients yet with her, it felt personal and heavy.

Eventually, their coaching relationship began to harm their marriage. Every conversation turned into a coaching session. Frustration built on both sides she felt judged, and he felt disrespected. Eventually, they sought marriage counseling to resolve the tension. It became clear that what worked professionally for him didn't work personally for them.

In the end, they both realized that he wasn't the right coach for her, and that was okay. Coaching someone you love deeply isn't always possible, because the personal connection can cloud objectivity. She ended up hiring me as her life coach instead. We worked together, set clear goals, and within months, she made remarkable progress. The best part? Their marriage improved too.

Sometimes, the healthiest thing you can do is bring in a neutral voice to guide the process.

If you are already in a situation where a spouse or family member is acting as your coach, it's worth having an honest conversation. Ask:

- Is this helping our relationship or straining it?

- Do I feel safe, or do I feel managed?

- Can we separate love from leadership without resentment?

Growth should strengthen your closest relationships, not strain them. Sometimes the most loving choice is to move coaching outside the relationship so that partnership, marriage, and family can remain places of rest, connection, and mutual support.

Choosing an external coach is not a rejection of your partner's wisdom—it's a protection of the relationship you're building together.

A New Season

Here is another truth I've learned over time: different seasons call for different coaches. The person who helped you get started might not be the person who helps you level up. And that's not a reflection of failure or weakness; it's just life. We grow, we evolve, and we need different perspectives at different stages. Think about professional athletes. Phil Jackson, one of the greatest basketball coaches in history, led the Lakers to multiple championships. His style was calm and strategic; he gave his players room to play, to think, and to find their rhythm. But not every player would thrive under his laid-back style. Some needed a tougher, more structured coach to push them harder.

I often tell my clients: *Don't hold on to a coach just because you've grown comfortable with them.* Comfort isn't the goal; growth is. If a coach has taken you as far as they can, it's time to thank them, honor the progress, and find the next person who can take you higher.

Each level of your journey will ask for something new from you: a new discipline, a new focus, new tools, and yes, sometimes a new coach. Staying open to that evolution keeps you growing.

The best coaches understand this, too. They don't cling to their clients or try to keep them longer than necessary. Instead, they celebrate their success, knowing that their work helped build the foundation for what comes next.

As I look back on my own journey, both as a coach and as a client, I see that the relationships that ended well were the ones that honored purpose over permanence. They taught me that every coaching connection has a reason, a season, and a lesson. When the reason has been fulfilled and the season has run its course, the lesson becomes your gift. So, if you ever find yourself in a position where a coaching relationship no longer fits, whether you're the coach or the client, take a moment to reflect. Ask yourself: *Has this season served its purpose?* If the answer is yes, it's time to close that chapter with gratitude.

When coaching ends with grace, both people walk away better. The coach grows wiser and more refined in their craft, and the client walks away stronger, more confident, and more self-aware. That's the beauty of coaching, it's not about dependence, it's about empowerment. It's not about staying forever; it's about learning enough to eventually move forward on your own. And when that happens, that's not the end of success, it's the proof of it.

.

CHAPTER 10

MY COACH, MY INSPIRATION

In life, there are certain people who don't just cross your path; they change the direction of it. They come in quietly, sometimes unexpectedly, but their presence leaves an imprint that stays with you forever. They are the ones who see the storm you're in, even when you try to hide it with a smile. They notice when your strength starts to fade and gently remind you that it's still there, waiting to rise again.

The one who sets your path in motion after you've been broken is not just a guide; they're a lifeline. When fear grips you so tightly that it steals your breath, this person stands beside you and says, "You can still move forward." They don't fix your problems; instead, they teach you how to stand tall in the middle of them. They show you that courage isn't the absence of fear—it's the decision to keep walking despite it.

In those moments when life feels heavier than you can bear, their voice becomes your anchor. They remind you of your worth, of your power, of the fact that no setback defines you. They teach through patience, compassion, and example. When you stumble, they don't judge; they extend a hand. And slowly, you learn to face the world again because the fear does not disappear, but because someone believed in you enough to help you believe in yourself. That's the kind of person who doesn't just touch your life; they transform it forever.

For me, that person is Dr. Sharon Rabb. Someone once asked me, "Of all the people you've ever met, who would you love to spend a day with?" I didn't have to think twice. My answer was simple: Dr. Sharon Rabb.

She didn't just teach me lessons; she modeled what grace, intelligence, and leadership looked like in action. Dr. Rabb had this rare ability to see potential before you could see it in yourself. She didn't just tell me I could do great things; she expected me to, and somehow, that made all the difference.

What stands out most about her isn't just what she accomplished but how she made people feel; she had a way of making you feel seen, valued, and capable. She didn't demand perfection; she nurtured growth. Her encouragement was never loud or showy; it was steady, consistent, and deeply personal.

Looking back, I realize that Dr. Rabb didn't just teach me to believe in myself; she taught me to be that kind of presence for others. To be the person who notices, who affirms, who lifts. Her example reminds me daily that one voice, spoken with kindness and conviction, can change the course of another person's life.

Dr. Rabb started out as my therapist in 2010, after an extremely tumultuous time in my life. I had lived a fairly unscathed life before that, and while I recommended and believed in therapy along with God, I had never felt the need to see a therapist myself. That year was different, and the circumstances that hit my life in that season threatened to literally cause me to emotionally crash. After a series of events, deaths, and betrayals, I realized that I needed to talk to someone to process what I was going through, as I was in a literal loop in my own mind with no answers or exit.

I got referrals, as I was pastoring a church, and the names of the people I would need to speak about in reference to what I was going through required a level of confidentiality that, for me, extended beyond the normal client–therapist relationship. I needed to feel secure and safe that this therapist could handle and hold information about people whom they might have known or heard of in the general societal news.

Dr. Rabb came highly recommended by two high-level industry people whom she had walked with through a high-profile situation and remained neither impressed by who they were nor dismissive of what they were going through. When we met, I was guarded and unsure of how she would be able to help me, but I went, knowing this was best for me.

Without going into the details, she started our sessions slow and let me ease my way into a level of comfort until I was able to open my heart and share honestly and without reservation. I have no words to describe how helpful she was, but I am confident in saying she had to be the best therapist I have ever known, and by profession and out of necessity, I know a ton.

As we were progressing toward a healthy version of me, one day, about a year and a half in, she said she wanted to inform me that our therapist–client relationship was ending. The panic that overwhelmed me in that moment was paralyzing. I felt someone finally saw me, heard me, and cared about me in a way that I had not experienced before. As my heartbeat was escalating, she could feel my trepidation and anxiety, and she quickly informed me that she was not leaving the relationship but ending the therapeutic part and wanted instead to move into a life-coaching relationship.

She reasoned that, under the therapist role, she was limited in what she could say, and her heart for my healing needed to have those boundaries removed so she could speak more freely. My heart rejoiced, my blood pressure returned to normal, and I gave her a resounding, "Yes, I would love that!"

Over the next year and a half, we became exceptionally close. She attended a few of my speaking events; I was invited into her home, and I met her kids and family. She coached me on how to avoid being codependent in my relationships, how to overcome my rescue-savior complex, and she exemplified coaching skills that literally saved my life.

If you have noticed, I have been speaking in the past tense, not only because it happened years ago but because the relationship took a shift when her cancer, the one she was just getting over when we started (in fact, I was the first client she took after being declared cancer-free in 2010), came back with a vengeance. Radiation, chemo, hair loss, a port in her chest, etc., were all a part of our final year.

By that point in time, I was family, and because the other calling on my life is as a pastor, I had the honor and privilege of walking her to heaven after she had walked me out of hell.

I owe a debt of gratitude to my cheerleader, coach, mentor, confidant, comrade, and champion, Dr. Sharon Rabb. Her legacy lives on in my work and that of her daughter, who is also a wonderful therapist. I wish everyone had a person in their life who, as the old African word denotes, in "Sawubona," says, "I exist because you see me."

I dedicated this book to her because she was the epitome of love and grace to me, and I would not have been able to operate in any of these 4 C's without her navigating between those roles in my life with fluidity and power. I exist today in a way I never would have had God not seen fit to add her to my life. I miss her greatly and look forward to seeing her one day in heaven and sharing how my life was better because she was in it.

Section III
Comrades

We Are Better Together

CHAPTER 11

COMRADES

Having cheerleaders and coaches in your life is essential—but there is another layer of support we often overlook: people who don't just encourage you or guide you but understand you. People who get you. That brings us to the next building block in building the team that builds you: comrades.

A comrade is someone who shares more than your journey—they share your risk. They understand you not just intellectually, but emotionally. Webster defines a comrade as "one with whom you have been involved in difficult or dangerous activities" or "a companion or associate who shares work, experiences, or purpose." At its core, comradeship acknowledges a simple truth: the idea that we can pull ourselves up by our own bootstraps is a myth. We were never designed to do life alone. We need people standing beside us—shoulder to shoulder—

through uncertainty, challenge, and the kinds of experiences that test our courage and conviction.

The word 'comrade' may feel old-fashioned, but its meaning is timeless and quietly powerful. We use different names for these people now—best friend, homie, ride-or-die, or, as my grandmother used to say, my "ace boon coon." Wherever the phrase comes from, it points to something real: shared history, mutual trust, and unspoken understanding. Comrades are the people who choose to walk with you through life's twists and turns—not out of obligation, but out of loyalty. They remind you that courage multiplies when it's shared and that even in silence, commitment speaks loudly.

A comrade is more than a friend. This relationship rests on three pillars: trust, empathy, and shared vision. Trust means you can be honest—even when the truth is uncomfortable or doesn't show you in the best light. Empathy means they understand not just your words but your silence—your emotions, your fears, your heart. And a shared vision means you are moving toward something bigger than yourselves, whether that's a cause, a dream, or personal growth.

Comradeship isn't born in comfort; it's forged in adversity. You discover your true comrades when life gets hard—when you're building something from nothing, leading through crisis, or trying to keep going when everything feels heavy. These are the people who don't disappear when things get messy. They roll up their sleeves and step into the storm with you. They don't ask,

"What's in it for me?" They ask, "What do you need?" There is something sacred about that kind of connection.

This isn't about shared hobbies or casual friendships—it's about shared hardship. It's about looking across the table at someone and knowing they see the same reality you see and feel the same weight you feel. Sometimes no words are needed—a nod, a look, or a quiet presence says, "I'm with you." That willingness to stand in the fire together is what binds comrades—not perfection or similarity, but commitment.

Comrades are mirrors of our resilience. They don't carry us; they walk with us. They remind us that the journey, no matter how difficult, was never meant to be traveled alone. When I look back on my own life, the people I call comrades are the ones who helped me find the strength I didn't know I had. They were the ones who showed up at my door and said, "Get in the car—we're going for a drive," when my thoughts felt tangled, and my hope felt thin.

You don't really know someone until you've walked through difficulty with them. And once you have, that kind of comradeship is often unbreakable.

I've learned that comrades rarely arrive with fanfare. More often, they emerge quietly—revealed in moments of pressure and uncertainty—when life makes it clear who is truly in your corner. They see your potential when you forget it. They stand with you when you feel alone. And in doing so, they help you keep moving forward.

CHAPTER 12

COMRADES & CONFIDANTS

As I wrote about comrades, I began to see how closely they can resemble confidants. The two share overlapping traits—trust, shared experience, and understanding—but they are not the same. Many meaningful relationships begin as comrades and, over time, some deepen into confidants. Understanding the distinction helps us honor each role without confusing its purpose.

Comrades often enter our lives through proximity, season, or shared purpose. They are the people who understand the grind because they're in it with you. They get the pressure, the pace, and the stress of what you're carrying, whether it's work, leadership, ministry, or a shared assignment. Comrades walk beside you during specific chapters of life. Many are seasonal by design, and when that season ends, the relationship naturally shifts or fades.

But occasionally, something deeper develops. When trust is built slowly, values align, and discretion is consistently demonstrated, a comrade may evolve into a confidant. At that point, the relationship is no longer anchored to a season—it becomes connected to your life story.

There was a season when I had neither a comrade nor a confidant, and I mistook isolation for strength. I wore self-reliance like a badge of honor, believing that carrying everything alone proved my capability. In reality, it was a false measure of importance. That mindset began to change when I met someone who showed me what a comrade-turned-confidant could look like.

We were initially connected by shared work and shared pressure. Over time, the relationship deepened. When I shared frustrations about the job, she didn't rush to fix me or offer advice. She simply sat with me, listened, and said, *"You don't always have to be strong."* That single sentence shifted my understanding of strength. I realized that having a confidant doesn't make you weak—it reminds you that you're human.

Comrades are often season-specific, formed through shared environments or experiences. Confidants, however, are rare. Their rarity is what makes them precious. Becoming a confidant requires time, consistency, loyalty, and discretion. When those qualities are proven, a comrade may transition into a bona fide confidant.

Confidants are the people you don't have to perform for. You can show up messy, unsure, frustrated, or tired, and they still see your worth. They hear what you don't say. They know when your silence is a scream and when your smile is covering pain. A true confidant tells you the truth in love. They celebrate your growth, but they will also say, *"You're better than this,"* because they believe in who you are becoming. And when life gets heavy, they don't disappear. They show up—with coffee, with presence, or with quiet companionship when words aren't necessary.

For me, being a confidant—and having one—means sharing a sacred bond rooted in trust. It's a space where someone has seen your worst and still chooses to stay. There's no need to compete, pretend, or explain. You can simply be. And in that kind of safety, healing begins.

I once read a quote—its author unknown—that has stayed with me because it captures this truth perfectly:

"Having a confidant means experiencing the inexpressible comfort of having to neither weigh thoughts nor measure words."

Comrades Who Become Confidants

There is a rare kind of relationship that goes beyond friendship—deeper than a casual connection and stronger than surface-level loyalty. These are the comrades who, over time, become confidants. They stand beside you not only when the sun is shining but also when storms arrive without warning. They don't flinch when life gets messy. Instead, they roll up their sleeves and walk with you through it.

A confidant isn't just someone who listens; they *understand*. They don't need long explanations to sense what's happening in your heart. You can say, "I'm fine," and they'll tilt their head and gently respond, "No, you're not." And instead of feeling exposed, you feel relieved—because you don't have to pretend. Sometimes you don't even have to speak at all. They feel when it's time to come close.

I've known people who loved the version of me that had it all together. But my true confidants? They stayed when I was falling apart. They spoke truth when I was too overwhelmed to see clearly. It's interesting how many people call themselves "ride or die" until life gets uncomfortable and they quietly disappear.

What makes a comrade-turned-confidant so rare is the blend of knowing, loyalty, and truth they bring. They won't let you spiral—but they also won't shame you when you do. I remember a season when I was exhausted, overwhelmed, short-tempered, and unsure of my next step. My confidant didn't offer a pep talk or a checklist. She simply said, *"You've carried a lot for a long time. Let me carry you for a while."* I almost didn't know how to receive that kind of love—it felt unfamiliar, but it healed something deep in me. That's what a comrade who becomes a confidant looks like: love in action.

These relationships are built slowly, over time. You can't force them, and you can't fake them. They're forged through shared hardship, laughter that turns into tears, and moments of honesty most people never get to see. A true comrade-confidant knows your history but doesn't hold it against you. They remember who you've been while still believing in who you're becoming.

The beautiful truth is this: you don't need many of them. If you have even one person who loves you enough to tell you the truth, remind you of your worth when you forget it, and sit with you in silence when words won't help—you are deeply blessed. We may have many comrades over the course of a lifetime, but comrades who become confidants are rare and often lifelong.

There is also power in *being* that person for someone else. When you move from comrade to confidant, you become a safe space for another soul. You offer what the world so often withholds: understanding without judgment, truth without cruelty, love without condition. For those of us who value independence and self-sufficiency, it takes courage to admit we need that kind of connection—especially if we've been betrayed before. Vulnerability is risky. But comrades who are also confidants remind us that life was never meant to be lived alone.

Most people fall into one role or the other. Comrades are easier to find. They appear through proximity and circumstance—work projects, school cohorts, shared responsibilities, or seasons of life. They often come and go. Confidants, however, tend to arrive unexpectedly. And when they do, something shifts. The noise of the world quiets a little, because you've found someone who sees you without needing explanations.

With a confidant, you don't have to "fake the funk," as my grandmother used to say. You can show up messy, frustrated, or worn out, and they don't look at you like you've failed—they nod, because they understand. They aren't shocked by your honesty. They don't panic when you say, "I'm scared," or "I don't think I can do this anymore." They listen—not just to your words, but to the truth beneath them.

They don't rush to fix you. They don't drown you in advice or motivational clichés. They let you exhale. Sometimes they sit in silence, knowing that healing comes from being seen, not solved. They help you untangle what's real from what's fear or exhaustion. They know when to say, *"You need rest,"* and when to say, *"Alright, it's time to get up."* And when they do, it's always with love, never judgment.

A true confidant will show up when you call in tears—no panic, no questions—just presence. They might bring snacks, tissues, or humor to help you breathe again. They may cry with you, laugh with you, or simply sit beside you until the weight lifts. And yes, they will also call you out in love. They'll tell you when you're playing small, when fear is talking louder than truth, or when you've forgotten your own strength. Not to criticize—but because they want to see you win.

Confidants are rare. Many people never experience that kind of connection. If you have even one in your lifetime, treasure them. They are the ones who walk with you through storms, who don't require explanations, who love you in your mess, and who remind you—even in your darkest moments—that you are not alone.

Sometimes a comrade evolves into a confidant. Other times, a confidant steps into the role of comrade and fights beside you when life demands it. Both roles matter. Comrades help you climb. Confidants remind you why you started climbing in the first place. One helps you win the battles around you; the other helps you win the battles within.

And when you have both, life becomes not just survivable but deeply meaningful.

Comrades Are Connected by Mission

It was important to me to make the distinction between the comrades and confidants because both are essential to building the team that helps you evolve into the powerhouse you were created to be. I've come to believe that comrades are joined together by a shared mission, a calling that goes deeper than personal comfort or gain. It's a bond built on duty, sacrifice, and purpose. True comrades don't gather because of convenience; they unite because something bigger than themselves demands it. Whether that mission is defending faith, protecting family, or standing for what is right in a world that often forgets truth, the connection is sacred. In my experience, you find comrades in every circle of life, in homes where fathers and sons work to build a legacy, in churches standing together against moral drift, or among civil rights activists determined to see freedom and liberty for everyone. Their loyalty is not to one person but to the cause they believe God has called them to serve.

As Ecclesiastes reminds us, "Two are better than one… for if either one falls, one can help the other up."

That's the heart of comradeship: strength found in shared purpose. Still, I've learned that such alliances are often for a season. Like scaffolding that supports a building during its rise, comrades help until the mission stands firm, and then they may move on. That doesn't lessen their value; it fulfills their purpose. These partnerships build character and courage, much like the early believers in Acts who worked side by side. History gives us countless examples: the Founding Fathers united for freedom, soldiers who stand shoulder to shoulder in battle, or community leaders who defend what's right even when it's unpopular. Comrades remind us that when people move with shared conviction, faith becomes action, and action shapes destiny.

Connected by Heart and Mission

I am reminded of the bond between the biblical figures David and Jonathan—a relationship that beautifully illustrates the movement from comrades to confidants. Scripture tells us that their souls were knit together, bound not by power, position, or convenience, but by covenant love. They stood as comrades in a righteous cause, united by shared purpose and mutual risk, yet they also became confidants—marked by soul-deep loyalty, trust, and protection.

Jonathan did more than fight alongside David; he armed him for battle and guarded his spirit. He offered both strength and safety, courage and compassion. That balance—of mission and heart—is rare, and it is powerful. I have seen it mirrored in strong marriages, lifelong friendships, and enduring partnerships that weather both triumph and trial. When both roles exist in one person, you gain more than support for the journey—you gain refuge along the way. You can share a vision, carry a burden, and still have a safe place to land when life grows heavy.

These are the people who will stand beside you in public and kneel with you in prayer when no one else sees. They will push you forward toward purpose while also reminding you when it is time to rest. This is strength— not the kind that dominates or demands, but the kind that sustains. When you are blessed to connect with someone who is both a comrade and a confidant, recognize it for what it is: a rare and sacred gift.

CHAPTER 13

COMRADES SHOW UP IN REAL TIME

In true companionship, comrades distinguish themselves with their unwavering dedication and trustworthiness, always demonstrating the qualities that make them reliable and dependable. This steadfast presence is not a matter of convenience but a hallmark of genuine character, rooted in discipline and mutual respect. There is a timeless parable that I refer to often when doing keynote speeches or when I need a good example of a comrade, friend, or confidant. I am not sure who the author is, and the characters often get changed out, but it goes something like this: A man (or woman) is walking down the street and, as they stroll mindlessly, tumbles into a hole, symbolizing the pitfalls of life encountered without foresight. They search and search but cannot climb out as the walls are slippery and without grooves, nor are they able to see another exit. They begin to yell and call out for help, hoping that someone is passing by and would be willing to help get them out of the hole.

Sure enough, as time passes, they hear someone passing by, and with increased urgency, they begin yelling, "Help, I have fallen into this hole, and I can't get out!"

Fortunately, it is a businessman who hears faint yelling and moves towards the hole, listening for the voice again. Upon hearing the panicked voice, he leans down and says, "May I ask how you got into this hole? Perhaps you need a better business plan or a strategist to help you avoid this kind of failure again. I know of a good one and I am sending her business card down. When you get out of this hole you can reach out to her!" A few more hours pass, and the hole occupant hears someone else passing by and begins yelling again. This time a therapist is the one passing by and yells down into the hole, "Why do you think you fell into this hole? Do you think it was your upbringing or childhood trauma that caused you to be careless with the direction of your life? I have a good book on how to overcome childhood trauma so you can avoid this kind of lapse in judgment again. Late in the evening, tired and feeling hopeless, the occupant hears another set of footsteps and yells with a panic-laced pitch. This time it is a priest who quickly runs to the hole and looks down with compassion and says, "My friend, my heart hurts that you have found yourself in such a horrible predicament. I will pray that you find your way out and that God blesses you with favor and grace when He finally delivers you!" The occupant hopelessly settles back onto the floor of the hole and ponders how long he may be in this space.

About an hour or two had passed when he heard a familiar voice calling his name. He yelled back, "I'm here, stuck in this hole." The voice came closer and leaned over—it turned out to be a comrade, a friend, a familiar face. Before he could say anything else, the comrade jumped down into the hole! Surprised and frustrated at the same time, the whole occupant says, "What have you done? Now we are both stuck in this hole!" The comrade's response says no, we aren't. I fell into this hole before, and I know the way out! This allegory underscores the value of comrades who intervene at critical junctures, perhaps pulling you back from the edge in the early stages or guiding you to safer paths later. Their timely presence prevents repeated errors, fostering resilience through shared vigilance. I love telling this parable because, upon hearing it, most people can relate to the relief and stress that is released when someone shows up and not only has the ability to help but is also willing to get into messy situations with us and walk us out.

The impact of having people who truly show up for you, those reliable allies who walk beside you through life, is far greater than we often realize. When someone is willing to stand with you in the middle of your mess, it changes how you carry your burdens. You feel seen, understood, and safe enough to be honest about what you're going through. That kind of presence is rare. It's not about them fixing your problems; it's about knowing you don't have to face them alone. When a comrade shows up, they create space for your feelings, a space where you can question, vent, and still be respected and loved. You can fall apart without fear of judgment. And in that space, healing begins. I've learned that when you have even one or two people like that in your life, the world feels less heavy. You start to believe again that tomorrow can be better.

Almost everyone can think of a time when everything seemed to fall apart; maybe you lost a job, a relationship, or even your sense of direction. Then someone appeared. They didn't come to give a speech or list all the things you should've done differently. They just sat with you, listened, maybe prayed with you, and reminded you that you still mattered. That simple act can pull a person back from the edge. It's what makes life bearable when everything else feels impossible.

True comrades don't just bring comfort; they bring clarity. Their honesty helps you see where you need to grow. They remind you of who you are when you've forgotten. But healthy comradeship is never about dependency; it's about mutual respect. You show up for them just as they show up for you. It's a two-way street built on trust, consistency, and shared values. In the conservative sense, I believe these kinds of relationships strengthen the very fabric of families and communities. When people show up for one another on time, with integrity, it restores faith in human goodness. It teaches responsibility and accountability. Frankly, that's what our world needs more of today: men and women who mean what they say, who keep their word, and who love others through action, not just talk. Comrades who walk with you through your hardest days don't just help you survive; they remind you how to live.

How To Know Who Is Who?

When it comes to comrades, I've learned that you can't rely on charm, quick chemistry, or a few good laughs. Real comrades reveal themselves slowly. I start by watching the small things, because small things tell the truth. Does this person show up when they say they will? Do they respond in a reasonable time, or do days and weeks pass without a word? I hold a simple standard: if someone is careless with little commitments, they will not stand firm in bigger battles. I am a firm believer that what people will do to other people, they will do to you under the right set of circumstances, because it is in their DNA to do so. I also test trust with tiny vulnerable elements of my life. I may share a light worry, not my heart, just a pebble, and see what they do with it. If it comes back to me from someone else, I take that as a quiet warning. Comrades, hold your words, even the small ones. Pretenders repeat them.

I also pay close attention to how they treat people when they think it doesn't matter. If a person is kind to me but rude to the waiter or the elderly, I know that kindness is selective. And selective kindness will not stand steady in a storm. Comrades show their character everywhere, not just when it benefits them. Over time, I ask myself simple grounding questions: Do we share respect for the same values, family, work ethic, and faith? I don't need a clone, but I do need someone who honors the same basics. I avoid people who crave attention, shift their stories, or become whoever the room needs them to be. A comrade has a backbone, not a stage script.

In my own life, I keep a small list of people I could call at midnight, whether my car broke down or my spirit did. That list stays small on purpose. Only those who have shown steady actions, not emotional highs, get added. I protect my peace by being slow to include and quick to observe. This isn't cold. It's wise. Comradeship is too precious to hand out carelessly. I don't need a crowd; I need clarity. I'd rather have one person I trust completely than twenty whose loyalty depends on convenience. Time has taught me that rushing relationships leads to disappointment, but patience builds the kind of comrades you can walk through fire with.

Betrayal Is Always Possible

I've lived long enough to accept a hard truth: because people are human, betrayal can come from anyone, even from people I once thought would never let me down. That's why I move slowly before I place someone in the circle of comrades. Comradeship may come through shared battles, but confidence is earned inch by inch. I don't hand over trust in one grand gesture; I place it like stepping stones and see how a person handles each one. I start with the simple things. If they honor the small things without being reminded, I pay attention. If they forget or give excuses, I adjust accordingly. Life taught me this the hard way. I once shared a personal family matter with someone I barely knew, and by the end of the week, it had traveled through circles I never intended. That moment changed the way I processed trust.

Now, I share in layers. Each layer represents time, consistency, and proof. I watch how a person treats people who can't offer them anything in return. I notice if they still have old friends, if they speak truth even when it's inconvenient, and if they stay steady when life gets messy. I lean toward relationships that grow naturally, church, community work, and daily routines because those are born out of real life, not opportunity. The intentional, strategic connections have their place, but they're often the first to crack when pressure shows up. So, I draw clear boundaries: this person is for fellowship, this one for work, this one for prayer, and this one for counsel. If someone tries to blur those lines, I step back before the damage hits. And when betrayal does happen, and it has, I let myself feel it, but I do not let it break me. I forgive where I can, but I also learn. I reset the boundary and keep moving. My heart stays open, but not unguarded. I welcome people in, but not before I see who's at the door and what they're carrying. That's not distrust; that's wisdom earned the long way. Now, for sure, there are some people in my life who operate in multiple lanes; their presence transcends one role.

Unfortunately, you cannot control whether someone decides to betray your trust or not, but you can take some steps to safeguard your heart as much as possible.

Safeguarding Your Heart

Proximity does not equal permission, and familiarity does not guarantee discretion. I've come to believe that trust isn't something you hand out just because someone seems nice, you are working together, or they say all the right things. It's something that must be proven, little by little, over time. Think of it like planting a seed. You don't sit down the next day expecting shade; you water it, tend to it, and wait to see if it grows strong enough to lean against. That's how I approach relationships now. Before I let someone into the deeper parts of my life, I watch the small things, nothing big, just enough to see how they handle their own responsibilities. Do they follow through without reminders? Do they treat it as important because I asked, or do they brush it off like it doesn't matter? Those little moments tell you a lot about how they may handle your heart.

I've learned not to make a big deal when someone doesn't meet my expectations of the relationship. But if a pattern develops, I just quietly adjust the level of access they get to my world. Not everyone earns a seat in the circle of confidants, and that's okay. Protecting your peace isn't being shut off; it's being wise. I've also noticed that the people who pass those small tests do it naturally. They don't need to be told how to be dependable; it's simply who they are. Over time, those steady, reliable souls become the ones I can call at midnight or lean on in silence. Building that kind of trust takes patience, but the reward is worth every bit of waiting. Don't you know where loyalty is rare and words are cheap? You should test trust quietly before giving it completely to someone, as it is one of the kindest things you can do for your own heart.

If I ever call someone a comrade, I pay attention to how they move when things get real. Anyone can clap from the sidelines when life looks polished, but a true comrade shows their character in the middle of the mess. I don't hand out loyalty badges on words alone; I watch their walk. Do they show up when the lights are not shining bright? Relationships like these are often forged in obscurity, slowly and faithfully.

Let me be clear, this isn't about testing people with suspicion terms; it's about discernment. A comrade's loyalty isn't built in a day; it's earned through seasons of showing up. It's simple: trust is proven in action, not talk. And when you find the few who've stood with you in battle and kept their integrity intact, hold them close. They're rare, and they make every mission worth it.

Oversharing Too Soon

There are times when we feel like we have met a comrade, and all the pieces fall together really quickly, and you feel like you "click." I'll never forget the time I opened up too quickly to someone I barely knew. We'd only known each other a few months, had a few good laughs over lunch, and in a moment that felt safe, I started sharing personal things, family struggles, and money stress, the kind of things you only tell people who've earned your trust. It felt freeing at first, like finally taking off a heavy coat. But two weeks later, pieces of my story were floating around in conversations that had nothing to do with me. It wasn't done out of cruelty, just carelessness. Still, it stung. That's when I learned one of life's quieter lessons: closeness takes time.

Oversharing too soon is like handing someone the keys to your home before you've seen how they treat their own. Real trust must be tested. These days, I remind myself that relationships grow in seasons. In the beginning, it's small talk and shared laughs that spring. As time passes and consistency shows up, you move into summer, the season of sharing hopes, ideas, and dreams. Only when someone has weathered storms with you, when they've proven they can keep your small secrets, do they get invited into autumn, where you share the deeper things: fears, failures, and faith.

I'm not guarded out of fear; I'm wise out of experience. Not everyone is meant to hold the weight of your story, and that's okay. Some people are companions for a moment, others for a mission, and a few are called to walk the whole journey. When you do find those few, the ones who handle your truth with care, those are the keepers. Because the ones who protect what you've shared don't just hear your story, they honor it. And that's where real friendship begins. built slowly, shared wisely, and guarded fiercely

Choose Wisely, Grasshopper!

I've learned over the years that not everyone who claps for you is truly for you. That's why I don't rush to call everyone "friend." I don't collect people to say I have a crowd. I'd rather have a few solid souls than a hundred names in my phone. Choosing carefully isn't pride; it's wisdom. It's knowing that peace is too precious to gamble with the wrong company. I pay attention to patterns, not promises. Do they keep showing up when it's inconvenient? How do they speak about others even when no one's watching? Are they steady, or do they shift depending on who's in the room? I've learned that integrity isn't loud; it's consistent. You can spot real character in the small moments: the person who shows up early to help set up when you are putting on an event or stays to help clean up after, the one who quietly checks in when you've gone silent, the one who prays for you without needing credit.

And I've also learned to listen to my spirit. Sometimes God gives you a nudge that someone isn't meant to sit too close, and that's okay. Not every connection is a covenant. Some people are in your life for a season, and some for the long haul. The key is discernment, learning to tell which is which. When I choose who to walk with, I ask myself, "Does this person add peace or drain it? Do they help me grow, or do they keep me small?" A good comrade or confidant won't compete with you; they'll cover you. They'll want to see you win, even when it doesn't benefit them. Those are the people worth keeping close. Building those kinds of relationships takes time, prayer, and patience. The right people don't just walk with you; they strengthen your walk.

Organic vs. Intentional Relationships

When I think about the people who've stood beside me in life's toughest moments, I can usually put them into two groups: the ones who showed up naturally and the ones I had to go looking for. The organic relationships are the ones that just happened. We met at church, through volunteer work, maybe while working late, while completing a corporate project, or perhaps standing shoulder-to-shoulder at a community event. We didn't start with an agenda or a let-connected mindset. Life threw us together, and over time, shared laughter, small favors, and quiet understanding built something solid. Those are my kind of comrades, the ones who prove themselves without trying. Then there are the intentional ones, the people I meet through work, conferences, or mutual goals. They come with purpose and potential. I respect those connections; some have turned into true partnerships. But I've learned to keep my eyes open. Intentional relationships can be fruitful, but they can also be fragile. When the project ends or the cause changes, so does the closeness. It's not betrayal; it's just reality. Some folks were meant to walk with you for a season, not a lifetime.

My heart leans toward the organic ones, though. The friends who've seen me tired, messy, unfiltered, and still show up anyway. The ones who call when they feel I'm off, even if I haven't said a word. Those bonds don't need constant tending; they've been tested by time, by trial, by truth. They're not built on what we can get from each other but on what we can be for each other. I still believe in being intentional when purpose calls for it. Sometimes, God sends help through those channels, but I never mistake purpose for permanence. The real comrades, the ones who weather both the storms and the silences, grow like wildflowers: naturally, steadily, and strong enough to last.

CHAPTER 14

A LOOK AT COMRADESHIP IN MOTION

Let me pull up a few well-known pairs that show what real comrades look like in action—people who showed up when it counted, held space when things got heavy, and proved the very points we've been talking about. They weren't flawless, and their choices weren't always perfect, but the way they stood by each other offers snapshots worth keeping in sight. These examples remind us that true support is built through consistency, presence, and shared intention, not grand speeches or slogans.

From my earliest childhood memories, Lucy and Ethel remain one of the clearest pictures of steady comradeship. They built their friendship the same way strong communities are built: through everyday faithfulness. Whether it was late-night rehearsals, early call times, or family struggles behind the scenes, they continued to show up for each other without excuses.

They protected one another's dignity, held each other's confidence, and offered a steady presence instead of drama. For young people today who often see friendships formed online and broken just as quickly, their example teaches something simple: real comrades show up in real time. They don't gossip, compete, or disappear. They stand beside you, not in front of you or behind you. Their legacy shows that trust grows through consistency, and loyalty is still powerful in any generation.

Ethel was a loyal comrade, a faithful sidekick to all of Lucy's outlandish ideas. The trouble they got into was more than comical; it was legendary, particularly when they were trying to get into one of Ricky Ricardo's shows. On one show in particular, Lucy posed as a male dancer with a full mustache, with Ethel as her female dance partner, desperately trying to get into the show. From the time they went to Italy and ended up stomping grapes together to trying to keep up with the chocolate candy conveyor belt and eating more chocolate than one could imagine, they did crazy things, and they did it together. Their camaraderie was legendary and extended off camera as well; the two moved from working comrades to longtime confidants!

Another duo who were powerful comrades was Mike Eisner and Frank Wells, who led Disney during one of its strongest decades, not because they were alike, but because they were very different but respected each other's strengths. Eisner was bold and creative, and Wells was financially astute and steady. One dreamed big; the other calculated wisely. Their partnership showed what happens when two people unite around a mission instead of ego. The lesson is clear: comrades don't always look the same, but they share values, discipline, accountability, and purpose. They show that teamwork grounded in trust can turn struggling seasons into strong ones. Their bond teaches young leaders that success is rarely solo; it grows when people build each other up, not tear each other down. The two helped build the Disney brand into a powerhouse in the entertainment industry. They increased Disney's market value from approximately 2 billion to over 22 billion during their reign, powerfully moving through what they called the Disney Decade with strategy and creativity that had rarely been seen on that level.

I was blessed to work for Walt Disney Imagineering during the Disney Decade and can attest to the rate at which we were pumping out rides, parks, movies, and new business. It was a phenomenal testament to two very different styles, utilizing their differences to collaborate and create wealth for stockholders and employees and safe, clean fun for families around the globe.

Now, admittedly, I am a Laker fan, and so I must mention the dynamic duo of Shaq and Kobe. More often than not, when people talk about Shaq and Kobe, they often focus on the clashes. And yes, they had them. Two strong personalities, two different approaches, and one massive spotlight. But when the ball tipped, none of that mattered. They locked in, focused, and dominated because their commitment to winning outweighed their disagreements. Their partnership shows a powerful truth: you don't need to agree on everything to achieve something great together. What you do need is shared purpose, discipline, and the maturity to put the mission above your feelings. Shaq and Kobe did that night after night, proving that real comradeship is built not in comfort, but in sacrifice, respect, and showing up for each other when it counts, leading to multiple victories.

How about comrades in the movie industry like Ben Affleck and Matt Damon? They built their friendship through years of shared struggle, long before success. They encouraged each other's talent, carried each other through financial lows, and guarded each other's private battles without broadcasting them. Their comradeship wasn't built on fame; it was built on trust, accountability, and shared vision. This is powerful for today's youth, who sometimes chase quick connections or overnight success. Their example beautifully illustrates how strong friendships develop gradually through patience, honesty, and mutual support. It's heartwarming to see that good friends not only bring joy but also help shape our character and guide us in positive directions.

CHAPTER 15

YOU WERE NOT MEANT TO DO LIFE ALONE

Can we do an honesty check? Have you ever had nights when sleep just wouldn't come? You lie awake with your mind racing, heart heavy, and a quiet fear whispering loudly. "You cannot carry all of this by yourself." I had a season like that, and one morning, I looked at myself in the mirror and saw a woman doing everything she could to keep the pieces together and losing herself in the process. That was the moment I remembered what I already knew deep in my spirit: God never intended us to live life in solitude. I read the Bible often for wisdom and direction, and there are scriptures in the bible that make it clear from the very beginning, before humanity ever faced temptation or struggle, that God never intended for us to do life alone. God looked at Adam, whole, healthy, surrounded by beauty, and said, "It is not good for man to be alone." That verse has anchored my perspective on doing life in and with community. If loneliness wasn't part of the original design, then community isn't optional. Needing one another was built into us from the start.

I learned the importance of that truth on the day I finally reached out. Life was "life-ing" hard, and I sent a message to two women I trusted. Nothing dramatic. Just, "Can we talk? I don't think I'm okay." I half expected them to cancel or say, "Sure, but maybe later." Instead, both of them were at my front door within the hour. No questions, no judgment. They sat with me while I tried to explain what felt too heavy. There had been so much going on; I wasn't sure what was really weighing me down. I let out all the emotions and frustrations I had been holding for months. They didn't preach. They didn't try to fix my life. They simply stayed. They held space for me. They reminded me by their presence that I was not carrying my burdens alone.

Simon Sinek, a powerful motivational speaker, author, and corporate organizational consultant, was on a podcast and told a story about a good friend who was going through something pretty dramatic, and he didn't know. He asked her why she had not told him, because as her friend, he would have wanted to be there for her and walk with her. She mentioned that she had texted him a few times to see if he had some free time, but her texts to him seemed like the usual casual texts of "What are you up to?" that she had sent a hundred times before. He said he didn't know it was a cry for help. So, they instituted what they call the 8-minute rule. If you need time or are in need of help, say, "Do you have 8 minutes?" as he determined that 8 minutes of intentional time listening and being present was often all someone needed to be heard, seen, and valued to know they were not alone.

That afternoon, my friends showed up for me, and it changed me. I realized that asking for help doesn't expose your weakness; it reveals your courage. Letting someone into the mess is not a failure of faith; it is an act of trust. It is admitting that God often answers our prayers through people who know how to stand with us. I think of my daughters when they fall or get hurt. They look for me first, not because I can erase the pain, but because being with someone makes the pain bearable. Adults are no different; we just think we are because we get better at hiding our bruises. We go through heartbreak, financial strain, exhaustion, and spiritual wrestling, and we tuck it all behind a strong face. But the need for connection never disappears. We still look for someone who will say, "I'm here. You don't have to do this alone."

Not everyone in your life will be a confidant, and that's perfectly fine. Many relationships are seasonal, some are casual, and some are meant for specific parts of your journey. But you do need a few, just a few, who know the unpolished version of you and love you through the good and the bad times. Those are your comrades. The ones who show up early, stay late, pray with you, sit in silence with you, and walk with you when the road feels longer than your strength. If you don't have those people yet, don't panic. You can start by being that kind of person for someone else. Send the check-in text. Follow up on the prayer request. Remember the doctor's appointment. Drop off a meal without making a big announcement. The most honest friendships grow from consistent, quiet care. When your own storm hits, those same people will show up, because real comradeship works in both directions.

Life was never meant to be carried alone, not the grief, not the joy, not the confusion, not the healing, not the victories. We were designed for connection, for porch lights left on, for heartfelt conversations, for shared courage, for shoulders to cry on, for laughter that breaks tension, and for community that steadies us when we feel unsteady. And when you finally let people in, really let them in, you discover something freeing: the weight lifts, the fear quiets, and the road becomes lighter simply because you're not walking it solo. So, make the call. Send the message. Let someone close. You were never meant to do this life alone, and once you stop trying to, you'll wonder why you ever carried so much by yourself.

Check On Your Strong Comrades

We must take a few minutes to talk about the comrades who show up for everyone else and never seem to falter or need anything. For many of us (yes, I said 'us,' as I fall into this category as well), being strong means staying silent. We keep smiling, keep producing, and keep solving everyone else's problems, but inside, we feel like we are fading out of our own story. The strong image keeps people from helping because we give the appearance that we don't need help. For me, sometimes I didn't want to risk someone not showing up and being disappointed, so I didn't ask, and other times I am so accustomed to carrying things on my own that it is just habit. We all need help, even if we have great capacity and strength. Just offloading some small stuff, which just might lighten the load a lot.

I've learned that human beings don't need grand solutions as much as we need honest recognition. We need someone who can look past our practiced smile and say, "I can tell this has been a heavy week." When that happens, even once, it has a way of steadying the heart. It reminds us that we're still visible, even when we feel like we've gone dim. I watch this with women all the time—strong women, capable women, carrying entire households, ministries, and careers. They move through life like pillars, holding everyone up, but longing for someone to pause and say, "I see you trying. You're not alone." And when someone finally does, you can almost watch the tension melt off their shoulders. Being seen is not weakness; it's nourishment. It tells the weary soul, "You matter, and I'm paying attention." Comrades do this effortlessly. They notice when your voice changes. They hear the fatigue you try to disguise. They sent a message at the exact moment you were praying someone would. They're not rescuers; they're witnesses. And sometimes being witnessed is the very thing that keeps us from slipping under the surface.

The truth is none of us outgrow the need to be seen. Even as adults, we move through hard seasons craving the same reassurance children do: "I see what you're carrying, and you don't have to carry it alone." When someone offers that kind of presence, it grounds us. It quiets the shame. It reminds us that we are human, not machines. So, if you're waiting until your life looks perfect before you let someone get close, you'll wait forever. Perfection isn't the requirement; honesty is. And the beautiful thing is this: when we finally let someone see the real, unpolished version of who we are, we make space for them to do the same. That mutual recognition becomes the beginning of healing, friendship, and, in the truest sense, comradeship. Because at the end of the day, none of us are meant to stand on our own island pretending we're fine. We're meant to be seen, known, and supported, especially in the places we try hardest to hide.

Comrades See Our Blind Spots

One thing I know for certain is that none of us sees ourselves as clearly as we think we do. I am sure you have had seasons where you believed you were handling everything just fine, only to learn later that you had missed something obvious to everyone but you. Blind spots don't show up like flashing lights; they hide in the habits we've carried for years, in the tones we don't hear, and in the attitudes we don't recognize until someone loving enough points them out. I remember a time when a close friend pulled me aside after a meeting and said, "Can I share something with you?" She didn't come with judgment. She came with care. She told me that lately, my stress was showing up as sharpness, especially toward people who didn't deserve it. I hadn't seen it at all. I was moving so fast, carrying so much, that I didn't realize how my words were landing. It didn't feel good to hear, but it was exactly what I needed. It gave me a chance to correct something before it caused real damage.

That's the thing about blind spots: we don't notice them because we're inside the moment. Our hearts don't always give us the full picture. Our emotions can make excuses. Our pride can whisper, "You're fine." And that right there is where the danger lives. Comrades help us see what we can't see. Not to shame us, but to protect us. They stand at the angle we can't reach and say, "I know you don't mean it that way, but here's how it sounded." They are not critics; they're caretakers. They love us enough to risk an uncomfortable conversation so we don't keep repeating something harmful. And when the message comes from someone who has proven loyalty and wisdom, it lands more softly. You can hear it without feeling attacked. I've come to believe that asking for feedback is not a weakness; it's maturity. These days, when I feel myself getting defensive, I try to pause and breathe. Then I ask the people I trust, "Is there something I'm missing?" I don't always like the answer, but I'm always grateful for it later. Their honesty has saved my relationships more times than I can count. We all have blind spots. Every one of us. That's why I believe God surrounds us with people who can see from a different angle so we don't keep stumbling over the same things in the dark. When we allow comrades to speak into our lives with love and truth, we grow. We get better. We learn how to move forward without hurting ourselves or the people we care about. And the best part? We don't have to figure any of it out alone.

Comrades Can Serve as Coaches and Cheerleaders

Maybe you have this issue as well. One thing I've come to understand about myself is that I can be a harsher coach than any person in my life. I can wake up already disappointed in myself, already convinced I'm behind, already rehearsing all the ways I should be doing better. It's amazing how quickly we can tear ourselves down before the day even begins. And right when my thoughts start heading in the wrong direction, one simple text will show up from a coach or comrade or cheerleader in my life: "Thinking about you today. Proud of you. Keep going." It's never long, never dramatic. But it resets me every time. That's the quiet power of a comrade.

Some people become comrades, coaches, and cheerleaders in your life without ever being asked. When I fall out of routine, whether it's skipping the gym or getting stretched too thin at work, they don't shame me or give me a speech. They just say, "I'll be at your house at 6. We'll go together." No guilt, just presence. That's coaching in the most respectful way: consistent, gentle accountability that lifts you rather than weighs you down. And then there are the days I actually do get it right. I wake up early, reach a goal, or finally follow through on something I've been putting off. I'll send a picture and a quick update while the encouragement pours in. It's funny how a simple "You did that!" or "Look at you showing up!" can carry you all day. It's not childish; it's fuel. It reminds you that progress, even small progress, deserves to be noticed.

A true comrade knows when you need truth and when you need celebration. Last year, I almost walked away from a project that felt too heavy. I vented to a friend about it, expecting sympathy. Instead, he said, "You're not tired; you're scared. Keep going. I'll check on you Friday." It wasn't criticism; it was clarity. And when that same project finally took off months later, he was the loudest voice cheering. One person, three roles, perfectly balanced. We all need all three. The coach part keeps us grounded when we drift. The cheerleader part reminds us why the fight matters. Left to ourselves, most of us default to criticism and forget to celebrate anything. But being surrounded by good comrades gives us a safe space to share our fears and apprehensions. The goal is to learn to do both, to show up for others and let others show up for us, and often they coach us to the next level of victory in our lives.

That's the beauty of these relationships. We get to exchange strength. When my friend was going through a rough season in his marriage, I started sending him the same late-night encouragements I used to get little reminders like "I'm with you." It wasn't about trying to fix him. It was about making sure he didn't walk that valley alone. Our life is long and unpredictable, and none of us is built to run it silently or in isolation. We need people who coach us with honesty and cheer for us with sincerity. People who see our best even when we can't feel it. People who celebrate our progress and stand firm when our confidence wavers. If you haven't had voices like that in your corner yet, don't lose hope. Start by being that kind of voice for someone else. Trust has a way of circling back to those who give it freely. Because at the end of the day, having comrades who coach you through the hard parts and cheer you through the victories doesn't just make the journey easier, it makes it worth taking.

Section IV
Champions

They Aren't Born, They're Made

CHAPTER 16

THE POWERFUL ROLE OF A CHAMPION

The final piece to this puzzle, the pillar that is often hardest to find and be, is a champion. I submit to you that we all, young, old, rich, poor, tall, or short, need a champion! Cheerleaders, yes, we need them. They push us forward. Coaches, yes, they are critical pieces to our journey, and we may solicit different types of coaches at differing points in our lives for the varying levels of our careers. Comrades are excellent to have in our corner, and over the course of a career or lifetime, several will be there to hold space for you in times of need. But a champion... well, in all honesty, I believe we need at least one in life to truly fulfill our destiny. You have heard it said it's not what you know but who you know. In some instances, relationship capital is better to have than degrees, experience, or money.

Champions are those who have a seat at the table already, who have a "heard and respected" voice in the room, and have the ability to speak up for you, recommend you, and pull out a chair for you to join the table. They see you; they believe in you and are willing to go to bat for you and risk their reputation because they know what you are made of, and they know your integrity and character that support your gifting.

A champion isn't just someone cheering from the sidelines or clapping the loudest when you cross the finish line. A champion is the one who walks into a room you didn't even know existed, sits at a table you didn't know had a chair for you, and quietly moves mountains on your behalf. In my life, I have had a few champions, and I want to share two stories to give you an idea of what a champion looks like in a small, seemingly unimportant context and another that was more direct, both of which shifted the trajectory of my life and career.

One small example: I worked 20 years for the Walt Disney Company at Imagineering, the division that designs and builds their theme parks. I got that job not because my resume was so stellar or because I fought hard to get into the company. No, it happened because after I had sent my resume in and it was filed away 3 years earlier, a friend I had worked with at another company happened to be in the HR office when they were ramping up staff for the Disney Decade in the 90's and pulled my resume out of a file. Someone in the office called out, "Does anyone know Andrea Humphrey?" My friend answered, although they were not talking to him, and responded that I was an excellent financial analyst and would be a great asset to the company. They called me, set up an interview, and I got the job and a huge raise, all because someone was willing to put their reputation on the line for me. The bulk of my professional career and the things that I learned about corporate culture, along with having a financially satisfying career, happened at Disney. He could have remained silent and not put his reputation on the line, but because he knew that I was good at finance, he didn't mind championing me at that moment. I worked on some of the most incredible projects from Disneyland to Disney World to Tokyo DisneySea and met some lifelong friends because someone was willing to vouch for me without being asked. Sometimes it happens as surreptitiously as that, and sometimes it is more strategic, more intentional. For instance, a friend of mine, Tyran Meredith, was/is an international speaker/pastor/teacher. He traveled all over the world as an expert on the intersection of ministry and the marketplace. In many of the countries he went to, the women could not be in the room with the men, and they would have to listen in another room via a speaker or not at all. Tyran would often ask if the women could come in, but culturally, it was not allowed. This really bothered him, and knowing my skillset was about the same as his, just from a female perspective, he reached out to me and said his plan was to bring me with him, and I would teach the women, and he would teach the men. As a result, I have spoken/taught in countries like India, the Philippines, and others because he thought of me in not just rooms but countries that I had never stepped into. It opened doors that, on my own, would have never been available. Champions are critical to your path forward, however it happens, circumstantially or intentionally.

Champions also protect your name even when you're not around. I've seen one champion shut down gossip about someone with four quiet words: "That's not who he is." Their word holds weight and gives credence and validity to your character. They invest real time in coffee dates that turn into two hours of strategy and text threads that start with "Saw this and thought of you." They don't keep score. They don't need applause. They act because they see your potential, and they know it's worth the risk, and the part that can still get me amped is a champion sees the version of you that you're too scared to see yourself. They know the book you haven't written, the business you're afraid to start, and the leader you don't feel ready to be.

Champions sponsor you. They elbow through crowded rooms, open doors, and pull you through even when your legs are shaking. Every promotion, every open door, every second chance I've ever received carries a champion's fingerprints. They act when no one is watching. They speak for you when you can't. They stand in the fire so you can walk through unscathed. So, I ask you, who is swinging the bat for you when you're not at the plate? And whose champion are you willing to be? Because the same hands that are being pulled up are the hands that should also extend downward. That's how it works: champions raising champions, doors opening, and no one ever climbing alone.

The Five Types of Champions

Let me break this down the way I would if we were really sitting together in my backyard sipping tea around the pool, just you and me, two glasses of sweet tea, and a great, provocative, energizing conversation. You with me? You know that moment when the sky turns gold, then orange, then that deep, quiet purple and blue? That's the kind of space we're stepping into right now. Because here's the truth I had to learn the long way: there aren't fifty kinds of champions out there. Not a hundred, not a complicated chart; you need a leadership seminar to understand. Just a few, and I have found five types that repeatedly come into view for me. These are the ones I have seen God use, sometimes gently, sometimes abruptly, sometimes in ways that knock the wind out of you to shape your story and push your life forward. And each type? They show up differently. Some walk into your life like a whisper. Some arrive like a door slamming open. Some stand steady in the background until one day you realize they held your whole world together when you didn't even notice the pieces were slipping.

And here's the wild part: once you start paying attention, once you *really* learn these five types and their attributes, something shifts. You stop brushing off the good people who cross your path because they don't look the part on the surface. You stop assuming kindness is random or that help is accidental. You begin to notice your blessings that show up in a champion in real time, not years later when you look back and realize, "Wow, I didn't even see what God was doing through them." When you know the types, you stop overlooking the people who are literally keeping your story alive. You start thanking them and God faster, appreciating, and holding the right hands a little tighter. And maybe, just maybe, you start becoming a champion for somebody else, too, because once you've been lifted, it's impossible not to feel called to lift.

Champion—Resource Providers

These are the people who somehow give you exactly what you need before you can even admit out loud that you're struggling or know what you need. They notice the worry in your eyes before you can find the words for it. I was lucky enough to have someone like that in my life, one of those quiet, everyday heroes you don't fully appreciate until later. When I was contemplating leaving my role at Disney after 20 years, I had already started my consulting company, I.Q. Training Inc., but had no clients yet. My boss at the time came to me and said, "I think you ought to quit and consult, as the things you want to do require more of your time, and you have a passion for teaching." She literally said, "I will hire you back as a consultant at your asking rate, and then all you have to do is come in to facilitate classes." It was as if she had read my mind and knew I needed a push to do it. She knew I was capable, and she knew that the thing I lived to do was teach and help people reach their potential. She was clear and persistent: you can do this and make more money than you are now, and I will vouch for you and push your contract through. She did everything she said she would, and not only did I get contracts, but I was able to parlay that into contracts at other entertainment companies.

She used her relationship capital to help resource me as a consultant after I was an employee.

Then there was a friend who heard that I had been invited to speak at a conference in South Africa, but I had to get there with my own funds and pay for my hotel. This happened right when I was hit with some major expenses in my other business, and it didn't make financial sense to spend money on that trip, given what I had to do with my company. Before I could even scramble for excuses, my phone buzzed. My friend sent the full amount on Venmo with a simple message that meant more than the money itself. I believe in you; go and help those people see that they can be and do more! See, resource providers are different. They don't just see where you are; they see where you could be. They notice the gap, the missing tool, the missing chance, and the missing confidence, and they fill it. Quietly and kindly. Without a spotlight, without strings, without needing the world to applaud their generosity, take a second and look around your own life. Who bought you the book that changed your thinking? Who handed you a contact that opened a door? Who gave you gear, tools, or even straight-up cash at a moment when your pride was too loud to even ask? That's them. That's your resource provider, and here's one thing I've learned the hard way: don't let their kindness fade into the fog of memory. Thank them now. Thank them while the moment is still warm. Some blessings deserve an immediate echo.

Champion—Mentors

These are the people whose wisdom was earned through real experience and hardship, the kind that leaves marks you can't always see. They sit with you, coffee in hand, honesty in their voice, offering truth you never asked for but secretly needed. Every so often, they tell you to bring your calendar and leave your pride at the door. They go through your goals, point out the weak spots, warn you about the wrong influences, and make you repeat the lessons they learned the painful way. Real mentors don't just give advice; they offer the shortcuts they carved out of their own failures. They recognize every pothole because they once fell into them and still carry the scars on their knees. They let their life experience paint a picture for you and help you see yourself in your own story. And when someone invests their time to strengthen your character, not just your résumé, you're receiving something rare. Treat that kind of guidance like an inheritance that can shape your entire future.

Champion—Coaches

Coaches are the ones right there with you in the trenches, clipboard in hand, and holding you to standards you didn't even know you had or could meet. They push with love and pull with accountability all at once. They notice when you're about to give up and won't let you quit without a fight. When you're avoiding the hard conversations or the uncomfortable work, they step in, guiding and correcting until you can face it with confidence. Coaches celebrate the discipline, the daily effort, the reps, and the consistency more than the trophies or accolades. They correct your form, sharpen your habits, challenge your mindset, and refuse to let you drift through your potential unnoticed. They talk you up to coaches at the next level, they tell others about your skill and what you are capable of, and they believe it. If someone is training with you across every part of your life, professionally and emotionally, they are a coach. And make no mistake: a coach is also a champion, quietly fighting for your growth and cheering you on when you're not even in the room. Cherish them, honor them, and feed that relationship with gratitude, because coaches who are champions are rare and invaluable.

Champion—Advocates

Advocates fight invisible battles in rooms you'll never even enter. They speak up for you when you can't, quietly clearing the path ahead. They shut down rumors before they spread, correct false impressions before anyone notices, and drop your name in conversations where opportunities are taking shape. They don't brag, they don't seek applause, and they act because your success matters to them. If people keep saying, "So-and-so speaks so highly of you," that is your advocate quietly doing holy work on your behalf. They are champions in every sense, defending and elevating you when you aren't even there to see it.

Advocates persistently work toward outcomes they believe are best for you. That could be going with you to the doctor after a negative diagnosis and asking questions you don't even know to ask. It could be talking to a recruiter about a position they know you would kill.

They even brag on your talent, skills, and character, which can open doors that you would not even think to walk through without their push. If you have an advocate, send them a short and sincere note of gratitude today; they'll never ask for it, but they'll feel it, and that's all that matters to a true champion.

Champion—Door Openers

These are the rarest of all. They don't just hand you a key; they unlock the door, push it wide, and pull you through, even when your legs are shaking and your confidence feels thin. A true door opener sees your potential before you do and bets their reputation on it. They spend political and social capital like it's nothing because they believe in the future you can't yet see. When someone risks their name to elevate yours, know that they don't have to but choose to. That is when you drop to your knees in gratitude, and you thank God for sending a door opener for you. Make it a point to make them proud; don't let them down by being less than they know you are capable of being. Their reward is seeing you succeed and knowing you took advantage of the door that was opened and walked through with power and grace.

Here's the truth: most champions wear multiple hats. Real relationships don't stay inside neat little categories. The same person can mentor you and open doors. Another can advocate and coach. Someone else can provide resources and cheer like they're front-row at your personal Super Bowl. The overlap? That's the real magic. So tonight, do something simple but sacred: Grab a napkin, jot down every name that fits one of these five categories, and send each person a quick note:

"Just thinking about how you've been a resource, provider, mentor, coach, advocate, and door opener in my life. Thank you. I'm still standing because of you."

Watch what happens when a champion realizes their investment landed; their joy and excitement are contagious. Finally, make a resolute decision to *be* one of these champions for someone, and if you don't think you are capable or have the resources, talent, position, or experience, ask God to help you see that you are capable, as there is always someone you can help. The hands that pulled us up are the same hands we're supposed to extend downward. That's how the whole thing keeps working: champions raising champions, doors staying open, and none of us climbing alone.

CHAPTER 17

WHO CAN SERVE AS CHAMPIONS?

Those who serve as champions for your goals are the individuals who step out of the shadows and stand beside you when the path ahead feels uncertain. Champions are not limited to one role or title. They may be mentors who offer wisdom shaped by experience, coaches who challenge you to rise beyond your comfort zone, trusted friends or family members who remind you of your worth, or colleagues and leaders who recognize your potential long before you recognize it yourself.

A champion is anyone willing to stand behind you when you feel discouraged, push you forward when frustration sets in, and help you rise above fear and the emotions that threaten to blur your confidence. They are present in moments of strength and in moments of breaking. They offer support when you are weary, nourishment when you are depleted, and steadiness when life feels overwhelming. Because of this, champions can emerge from many places—anyone with a sincere heart and a genuine desire to see others thrive.

What distinguishes a champion is not proximity, but intention. They believe in your journey not because they expect something in return, but because they are invested in your growth. Champions offer guidance when your direction becomes unclear, share resources when your capacity feels limited, and provide accountability when self-doubt tries to cloud your vision. Their encouragement lifts you. Their honest feedback helps refine you. And at times, they leverage their influence to open doors you didn't even know existed.

Whether through a timely conversation, a strategic opportunity, or a quiet reminder of your purpose, champions support more than your success—they fuel your transformation.

Respected Voices

A champion isn't just someone who claps for you from the sidelines; it's someone who can open doors you cannot open on your own. When we say a champion is someone "who has a seat at the table," we're talking about individuals who already hold influence or authority within a space. These are the people who can speak your name in rooms you haven't entered yet. Their voice isn't just heard; it's valued. And because of that, when they advocate for you, the impact is real. A person with a respected voice may not necessarily be the loudest person in the room, but their presence carries weight. They've built trust. They've shown consistent judgment.

Others turn toward them when decisions need to be made. When that kind of person decides to champion you, it can change the trajectory of your opportunities. Why? Because their words act like a stamp of credibility on your potential.

I remembered that day when I was on a flight from Nigeria not too long ago, seated beside a gentleman who carried the kind of calm confidence that only decades of experience can carve into someone. As we settled in, we exchanged a few simple pleasantries, nothing more than the kind of small talk that usually dissolves once the plane levels out. But this time, it didn't fade. I learned that he was a consultant for Price Waterhouse Coopers, and not just any consultant, but one who had built an extraordinarily successful career and was just four weeks away from retirement. There was a gentleness in the way he spoke about those years, as if he held both pride and gratitude at the same time. Naturally, I asked the question I always ask people who have run their race well: "Who was your champion at the beginning?"

He paused the way people do when a question brushes against something meaningful. A few seconds passed, then he smiled and began to tell me a story. When he first joined the firm, he and another young consultant, both talented and both inexperienced, were being considered for a high-end client. It was the kind of client that could shift a person's entire career if handled correctly. Neither of them had yet been tested at that level. Their boss invited both men to lunch. Not a formal interview and meeting, nor a high-pressure performance evaluation, just lunch.

But as he remembered it, the boss spent the whole meal asking what he called questions that dug a little deeper and slowly revealed his values, work ethic, and potential. There was no hint of favoritism. The boss listened evenly. Observed quietly, measured carefully. At the end of the meal, he thanked them both and simply said, "My decision will be coming soon." A few days later, the call came. The boss had chosen him. He told me he wasn't entirely sure what tipped the scales. In his mind, the other candidate was just as capable, just as hungry, just as ready. But the boss saw something, some spark of promise, some unseen potential, and decided to take a chance on him. From that moment on, everything changed. He excelled with the client. Exceeded expectations. Earned trust and delivered results without even realizing it at the time, he stepped onto a new trajectory, one that would shape the next few decades of his life.

Then he said something that stuck with me long after we landed: it wasn't just that my boss championed me. It was honoring his faith in me by performing well. His belief opened the door, but my work kept it open. That is the quiet truth most people miss. A champion doesn't carry you. A champion positions you. But what you do with the opportunity multiplies the power of that champion. Your excellence becomes their credibility, your success validates their decision, and your performance turns their risk into reward.

In return, the circle expands outward: the young consultant who rose, the boss whose discernment proved right, the client whose needs were met, the company that benefited, and eventually the next generation of people he would go on to champion. Did you catch it? Most people don't. They hear the story and stop at "A boss took a chance on him." But the real beauty goes deeper than that. It is the partnership between a champion's belief and a worker's excellence. It is the realization that being championed is not the finish line; it is the starting gate. It is the understanding that when someone invests in you, you honor that investment by showing up fully prepared to rise. The truth is simple but powerful: a champion opens the door, your performance walks you through it, and together, the two of you create momentum that lifts not just your future but the futures of everyone connected to the opportunity.

They See Your Work and Work Ethic

Champions are not always those sitting in a high-level executive chair. Sometimes the most powerful champions are the people who literally work beside you, the ones who have watched you show up, put in effort, push through challenges, and stay committed even when things get tough. These are the people who know your work from the inside, not from a distance. A champion who truly knows your work ethic speaks with authenticity. They've seen the late nights, the extra effort, the attention to detail, and the ways you step up without needing applause. They understand the heart you put into what you do. That firsthand knowledge makes their support incredibly credible.

These champions aren't just impressed by what you produce; they are impressed by *how* you produce it. They notice the consistency. They notice the discipline. They notice the growth. People who know your work ethic are champions who advocate based on truth. They can say, "I've seen how they handle pressure," or "I've watched them bring calm into difficult situations," or "I can vouch for their character because I've worked with them closely." That kind of endorsement carries weight because it's rooted in lived experience, not assumption.

These champions can accelerate your growth in two ways: First, they tell the truth about your strengths when you might talk yourself down. And second, they help correct the misconceptions others may have about you, especially in environments where bias, misunderstanding, or invisibility occur. Another reason champions who understand your work are so valuable is that they often spot opportunities that fit you. Because they know your style, your abilities, and your personality, they can recommend projects or roles that align perfectly with where you shine. And here's the best part: they keep you grounded. Champions like this may cheer for you, but they also challenge you. They can say, "You can handle more," or "You're capable of better." Their belief comes with honesty. It's growth-oriented, not just comforting. These aren't people who champion you blindly. They champion you because they've watched you earn it day by day. Let's look at a few people who should know your work and your work etiquette.

Bosses—When Leadership Becomes Championship

A boss can simply manage your tasks, sign your evaluation, and keep the machine running. Or, if you're fortunate, they can become something far rarer: a champion. Not the cheerleader type, but the kind of leader who stands up with quiet strength and puts their credibility behind your potential. A champion boss doesn't just notice your work; they understand the story behind how you work. They see the grit behind your calm, the late nights behind the polished results, and the ambition behind your silence. A true champion boss is someone who wants to grow people, not control them. You can feel the difference immediately. They don't micromanage you to death or make you walk on eggshells. Instead, they offer structure that invites you to step into your capabilities. They challenge you in a way that makes you rise, not shrink. They speak truth you may not want to hear but always need. They celebrate wins you overlook and correct you without humiliation.

This kind of boss not just hears but listens, really listens. They take time to learn how you think, how you solve problems, where your confidence dips, and what fuels your drive. Their mentorship isn't generic. It's deliberately shaped around you. A champion boss knows when to step back and let you lead an idea and when to step forward to shield you from unnecessary harm. They understand that leadership is not about sitting above others but about lifting them. They talk about your strengths when you're not in the room. They bring your name into conversations where opportunities are being discussed. They recommend you for roles you never thought you were ready for because they see ability in you before you fully recognize it in yourself. When they speak for you, their words carry weight because everyone knows they don't gamble their reputation lightly.

You may work for many managers in your life, but you'll never forget the boss who believed in you before the world did. The one who saw more in you than you knew how to articulate. The one who held open a door wide enough for you to step through with courage. If you've ever had a boss like that, you know their impact never leaves you. And if you haven't yet, trust that one day you will, and when it happens, it will feel like someone finally turned the light on in a room you've been walking through in the dark.

We don't talk about this often, but there are times when the people around us see our power and influence and are intimidated by our talent and gifting, and they are afraid that if they pull up a chair for us, we may take their spot, and we may become their boss! So, as opposed to getting offended and feeling like they blew you off or were unwilling to support you, we have to be careful that when people don't operate in the way that we think they should or open doors for us that we believe they have the capacity to open, we don't take it as a sign that we don't have value. How you respond to a "no" may be the key to a yes down the line.

Friends—The Champions Who Hold Your Spirit Together

A friend who becomes a champion is a rare blessing. Not every friend earns that distinction. Some people enter our lives for convenience, some for a season, and some simply because life places us in the same space at the same time. But a friend who champions you chooses you—again and again—through bright seasons and stormy ones, with a loyalty that doesn't need to be loud to be powerful.

Champion friends see you without performance. They know the version of you that doesn't have to be polished for work, poised for strangers, or strong for family. They witness you in the uncertainty, the broken confidence, the quiet hope, and the quiet fear. And instead of retreating, they stay. They create space for you to breathe without judgment and remind you that you are not too much, not too little, not too late—you are human, and that is enough.

One of the clearest lessons I've learned about champion-friends is this: support does not always look like access, and loyalty does not always come in the form we expect. As I mentioned earlier, one of the times I was stuck in a self-limiting space, I met with my friend to ask if she would be willing to help me get into a new space of creativity and opportunity. I wasn't asking for the spaces she was occupying, but introductions into environments that I did not have access to but knew were in the path of the next phase of my life's journey. My friend was affirming and encouraging, warm and engaging.

However, she did not see herself opening the door for me in the spaces she had access to. Instead, she mentioned other things she saw me doing with my talents, which were not where I thought I wanted to move into. It was a good meeting, and my friend had some great ideas, but it wasn't what I was asking. It would have been easy to be disappointed, but I saw the heart of my friend, who did not see herself as able to introduce me into those spaces but did see my potential and validated it. Later, I was able to realize she was not settled in her own perspective of herself and saw herself as still climbing without the ability to bring others along with her yet. We must be really careful that we don't feel entitled, believing those who "know us" should automatically lend their name, resources, or influence to us because we are friends. I appreciated my friend's help for what it was and left the meeting without resentment or a busted expectation.

A friend who champions you isn't impressed by your résumé. They're impressed by your resilience. They admire your capacity to grow, to feel deeply, and to try again after disappointment. They are the people who know your history but refuse to limit you to it. They hold your past gently without using it against you. When you fall apart, they don't panic. They stay. They understand that sometimes what you need is not advice, but presence.

Friends also champion you in silence. They, too, defend your name in rooms you aren't in. They correct people who misjudge you. They protect your reputation when others try to twist your story. They don't entertain gossip that diminishes you. Even when you don't know what's being said behind your back, they're there, safeguarding your dignity with a fierce kind of loyalty. A friend once told me that they were in a car with a few other leaders, and my name came up, and one of the men in the car said, "Oooh, I heard she was a dragon lady!" My friend, without hesitation, asked that person if they had ever met me, and they said no. He asked if he had ever talked to me on the phone, and the same answer was no. He then asked what would make him give negative commentary about someone he had never met or witnessed or had any verifiable information on. The man stuttered and started backtracking his commentary. My friend silenced the car by noting that to give an unsolicited negative view of me and potentially poison the other leader's perspective of me was wrong and lacked integrity. The man apologized and admitted that what he had heard was gossip and would not make that mistake again about me or anyone else. That friend was a champion of my reputation in a room I was not present in! What makes a champion friend's support so meaningful is that it's voluntary. They owe you nothing. They aren't bound by blood or paycheck or obligation. They are in your corner because they choose to be, because something in your soul resonates with theirs. That kind of connection is a gift, one you don't stumble upon often.

When a Sibling Becomes a Champion

Sometimes the loudest champion in the stands isn't a mentor, executive, or gatekeeper—it's a sibling. Not just because of shared DNA, but because siblings witness what most people never see. They see the blood, sweat, and tears. They know the late nights, the setbacks, the frustration, and the moments when quitting felt easier than continuing. Their belief is built on proximity and history, not hype.

A sibling champion has a unique credibility. They remember who you were before the title, before the applause, and before the breakthrough. They've seen you fail and get back up. They've heard you doubt yourself behind closed doors. So, when they cheer, it carries weight. It's not admiration from a distance—it's belief rooted in knowing your full story. In fact, my youngest daughter is a dancer, and the joy would rise up when my oldest daughter would go to her sister's meets and cheer like crazy because they shared a room, and she knew more than anyone the times when her sister wanted to give up or thought she was not enough.

Siblings often cheer in practical ways, too. They show up when no one else does. They remind you of your strength when your memory gets short. They advocate for you in rooms you'll never enter, not because it benefits them, but because they want to see you win. And when the world finally applauds you, a sibling champion is often the one clapping the hardest—not out of surprise, but out of confirmation. *They knew all along.*

Not every sibling relationship is perfect, and not every sibling can be a champion. But when a sibling chooses to stand in that role, it is a powerful gift. Their support is layered with loyalty, shared history, and love that predates success. A sibling champion doesn't just celebrate the win—they celebrate the journey it took to get there.

And if you are that sibling for someone else, never underestimate the impact of your voice. Your encouragement carries a depth others can't replicate. You're not cheering for potential—you're cheering for perseverance. That kind of championing leaves a mark that lasts far beyond the moment.

Parents—The First and Loudest Champions

Parents, whether biological or adoptive, often become the earliest champions in our lives, long before we understand what the word even means. Their support may not always be perfect, and their methods may not always fit who we eventually become, but at the core, a parent's love is rooted in an unshakeable desire to see you well, whole, and supported. And that kind of foundation shapes everything that comes after. A parent's championing begins before you ever achieve anything. They believe in your worth simply because you exist. They see potential in you when you're still figuring out how to understand yourself. They frame your earliest understanding of safety, belonging, and courage. A parent's support can plant seeds that take decades to bloom: confidence, empathy, and the quiet certainty that you matter.

Parents champion you through their presence. Even when they can't fix your problems, they show up. They show up in ordinary, unnoticed ways, packing lunches, checking in, giving advice you roll your eyes at but still internalize, and offering comfort when the world outside feels cold. That presence, even when imperfect, becomes the emotional baseline you return to throughout your life. Recently, my youngest daughter went to a teen leadership transformation summer camp. The camp was held high up in the San Bernardino mountains, off the beaten path, where there is no cell phone service. As you may already be imagining, this was going to be "torture," according to my daughter, not to have access to social media for 4 WHOLE days!

This note is important because it also meant I could not check in with her to find out how she was doing or what she thought about the camp and the program's agenda. At the end of the four days, her dad, older sister, and I went to pick her up, anxious to find out how transformational the camp had been for her life. We met with the leaders of the camp first and were debriefed on what they did over the course of the camp, and we were encouraged to ask questions if we needed to. After the debrief, the kids entered the room and sat on the floor in front of the room, facing the parents who had come. We had already been briefed that any of them who wanted to share their experience or anything with their parents or the group would be encouraged to just stand up and say what they wanted to say. One by one, they stood up, sharing promises, commitments, or revelations they received over the course of the camp. When a kid would stand to speak, the entire kid group would erupt with cheers of encouragement and affirmation, giving the speaker confidence to share. All of them cried as they spoke and were handed tissues or a reassuring hand or back rub as they struggled to share very vulnerable emotions and thoughts.

For the sake of not being throttled by my kid or embarrassing her, I won't share what my daughter spoke on, as that was private and she would kill me lol. However, there was one kid who grabbed my attention and made me think of this concept of champions. She started out with an exceptionally quiet, soft voice that trembled with a certain level of unassured confidence as she spoke. Her eyes searched the crowd and landed on her dad, and the unsure crease in her eyes softened and was replaced with a humble boldness that began to give her courage. She stared at him, seemingly seeing no one else in the room, and began to express how much of a champion he had been in her life. She spoke of his constant encouragement and wisdom, his ability to give her correction without crushing her, and his love that allowed her freedom and yet had enough guidance that if she strayed too far off course, she could course correct. She thanked him for being at all her sporting events and told him how much that support meant to her. She ended by saying that during the camp, she realized much of what she learned there was simply reinforcing what he had been teaching her throughout her life and how it propelled her to want to lean even more into his counsel and love. Her final thought was how much she loved wearing his college numbers on her sports jerseys to represent him and how proud she was to have his last name, and she always endeavored to make him proud, yet knew that he was already proud of her for just being her.

To say there was not a dry eye in the room is an understatement! I was almost afraid to look back at her dad, for I thought for sure he would be on the floor, sobbing at her eloquent description of the ways he had championed her. I snuck a quick peek, and sure enough, his eyes streamed with tears and pride as he listened to his daughter, and I realized in that moment not only had he been a champion in her life, but she was, in that moment, being an amazing cheerleader for his efforts at being a good dad, and each of us was afforded an opportunity to be inspired and pushed to be all of that for those in our lives.

A parent's voice is unique. It can calm storms you didn't even realize you were carrying. It can challenge you in ways no one else dares. It can remind you of who you are beyond your accomplishments. Parents have this deep, instinctive understanding of your core; they know your spirit, your sensitivities, and your patterns. They recognize your sadness before you speak it. They sense your joy before you express it. And when they see you drifting away from yourself, they gently pull you back. Parents, in their truest form, are the quiet architects of your confidence. They build the emotional scaffolding that allows you to rise, fall, and rise again. They teach you how to love, how to be loved, and how to build a life with courage.

CHAPTER 18

BEWARE OF THE IMPOSTERS

Not everyone who stands near you is standing for you. As you grow, heal, shift, or achieve, you will naturally attract two kinds of people: true champions and quiet impostors. Champions invest in your rise. Impostors are unsettled by it. Champions amplify your voice. Impostors imitate it—or attempt to silence it. Champions celebrate your wins with sincerity. Impostors offer surface applause while privately struggling with your progress.

Impostors rarely announce themselves. They often appear as helpers, collaborators, teammates, or even friends. On the surface, they seem supportive—but over time, their energy reveals otherwise. They may feel threatened by your confidence, uneasy about your potential, or intimidated by the way you elevate spaces simply by being yourself.

Understanding impostors matters because champions are best recognized by contrast. You learn the value of genuine support only after encountering support that was performative. You understand the power of real advocacy once you've experienced what it feels like to be quietly undermined. Discernment is not suspicion—it is wisdom earned through observation.

Be especially cautious of individuals you assume could be champions but who are still unsettled in their own journey. Their intentions may not be malicious, but their instability can cost you time, momentum, and resources. When they engage, the appearance of help often outweighs the substance of it.

When evaluating whether someone has the capacity to truly champion you, watch for these indicators:

- They make promises but fail to follow through.

- They initiate support without sustaining it.

- They speak confidently but produce no tangible results.

- They appear to have influence or authority, but lack real decision-making power.

- Their advocacy benefits them more than it supports you.

- Their help comes with conditions that feel transactional, manipulative, or excessive.

Impostors come in many forms, but three are most common: competitors, jealous friends, and insecure coworkers. Each one reveals something—not about your worth, but about their own unresolved tension. Let their behavior teach you discernment, not bitterness, and remind you of the kind of champion—and human—you never want to become. Remember, discernment protects what destiny requires.

Imposter Competitors

A healthy competitor pushes you to grow; an insecure one pushes you to doubt yourself. Imposter competitors aren't interested in mastering the standard—they want to beat *you*. Their motivation isn't excellence; it's comparison. They turn everything into a silent contest, even when you never agreed to compete. At the core, their behavior reveals a deeper truth: something about your presence threatens the version of themselves they are trying to maintain.

Imposter competitors watch you closely. They study your wins the way someone stares through a boutique window—wanting what they see while resenting the price you paid to earn it. They mimic your strategies, adopt your tone, and replicate your work ethic, not out of admiration, but out of urgency. They aren't asking, *How can I grow?* They're asking, *How can I catch her?*

Here's the quiet reality: they see you as the standard, even if they pretend otherwise. You are not competing with them, but they are competing with you because it soothes their insecurity. They don't celebrate your wins; they measure them. Compliments are brief, applause is delayed, and support is conditional, offered only after they've ensured your success doesn't overshadow their own.

A true champion lifts others; an imposter competitor tries to pull you sideways. Over time, I learned to stop measuring myself against anxious, performative energy that focused more on keeping up than learning. Their insecurity said nothing about my worth—it only revealed their limits. I outgrew them not by winning, but by refusing to play a game that was never mine to begin with.

Jealous Friends

Jealousy in friendship is one of life's quiet heartbreaks. It's subtle, confusing, and painful—because we expect friends to champion us by default. But not every friend is built for your evolution. Some were comfortable with the version of you who doubted yourself. Some felt secure when your dreams were still whispers instead of realities. When you grow, jealous friends don't grow with you—they grow distant.

A jealous friend rarely attacks openly. Their sabotage is quiet. They cheer publicly but question you privately. They downplay your accomplishments, attribute your progress to luck, or shrink your dreams into something impractical. Their discomfort isn't rooted in hatred—it's rooted in exposure. Your growth forces them to confront the courage they haven't yet found in themselves.

Jealous friends cannot be champions because champions want you to win, even when they are still waiting for their own breakthrough. They celebrate your shine without comparison. They aren't intimidated by your progress because they are secure in their own path. Jealous friendships teach you discernment. They help you distinguish between those who applaud your heart and those who only tolerate your performance. And when you step back from a jealous friend, you eventually realize their distance was not a loss—it was clarity.

Insecure Coworkers

Insecure coworkers and bosses are among the most draining impostors because they operate close to opportunity—and sometimes power. Their insecurity makes your competence feel threatening. Your confidence feels like competition. Instead of collaboration, they default to control.

These impostors function from a mindset of scarcity. They believe success is limited: if you rise, they fall; if you shine, they dim. As a result, insecurity often shows up as subtle sabotage—information withheld, meetings missed, ideas taken, and guidance intentionally unclear. Their goal isn't excellence; it's survival. And when someone is in survival mode, everyone around them feels like a threat.

True Champions	Impostors
Celebrate your growth without comparison	Measure your growth against their own
Amplify your voice and vision	Imitate or attempt to diminish your voice
Are you secure in your own journey?	Are you unsettled by your progress?
Advocate with integrity, even when you're not present	Appear supportive but undermine quietly
Offer guidance without conditions	Attach hidden costs to their help
Are invested in your growth, not their image	Are invested in proximity and perception
Lift others willingly	Compete, control, or sabotage subtly
Operate from abundance	Operate from scarcity
Protect your reputation	Benefit from your exposure
Want you to win—even if they're still waiting	Want to win because you're winning

Insecure bosses are even more complex. Their authority becomes armor for their self-doubt. Instead of mentoring, they micromanage. Instead of empowering, they belittle. Rather than championing your strengths, they focus on containing them. But their behavior is not a reflection of your capability—it is a reflection of their fear.

These impostors teach you what leadership is not. They reveal how dangerous authority becomes when the ego goes unmanaged. They remind you that titles may grant power, but character determines influence. Though painful, insecure coworkers often strengthen you—building resilience, clarity, courage, and self-trust. In contrast, true champions in the workplace become unmistakable. You recognize integrity faster. You value guidance more deeply. And you protect your purpose more fiercely.

Discerning between champions and impostors is not about cultivating suspicion or closing yourself off from connection. It is about wisdom, not walls. Every relationship does not fail because someone is malicious; many fail because expectations were misplaced. Not everyone who walks with you is meant to carry you, and not everyone who supports you is meant to support you in every way.

This understanding invites grace—for others and for yourself. People can care deeply and still lack capacity. They can love you and still be limited by their own season, fear, or growth. Recognizing this does not require resentment; it requires clarity.

As you move forward, the work is not only discerning who belongs in which role but also learning how to manage expectations with honesty and maturity. When expectations are aligned with reality, relationships breathe. Disappointment lessens. Resentment fades. And space is created for healthier, more sustainable connections.

The next step, then, is not just identifying champions—but learning how to hold every relationship with appropriate expectation, grace, and wisdom.

CHAPTER 19

MANAGING EXPECTATIONS: THE CARE

FRAMEWORK

When expectations are managed wisely, relationships are freed to be what they are—without carrying the burden of what they were never meant to be.

For a long time, I believed that the people I cared about most would automatically champion me. I assumed proximity meant support, and history guaranteed advocacy. I expected familiar faces to cheer me on, speak my name in the right rooms, and step forward when opportunities appeared. That assumption cost me more disappointment than I anticipated. Rejection hits differently when it is silent, when it isn't what they say but what they don't say. It can make you question yourself, your talent, and your relationship, and if you stay in your feelings, it can set you back or even worse, paralyze you for a period.

Over time, I learned a liberating truth: support is a choice, not an obligation. People are complex. Their confidence fluctuates, their emotional capacity shifts, and their vision of what's possible doesn't always expand at the same pace as yours. When people I counted on stayed quiet or distant, it hurt—and I took it personally. But growth taught me something freeing: I cannot force someone to champion me. What I can do is learn how to manage expectations wisely.

That wisdom became clear through four essential practices that are easy to remember and implement:

C—Clarify Capacity

Not everyone who cares about you has the capacity to support you.

This was one of the hardest truths for me to accept. Some people love you deeply but lack the emotional maturity, professional stability, or internal confidence to champion anyone else. Their silence is not always rejection—it's limitation.

Once I learned to separate intention from ability, disappointment lost some of its sting. I stopped assuming that care automatically translated into capacity. Clarifying capacity helped me understand that unmet expectations often reflect someone's limitations, not my lack of worth.

A—Assign Roles Accurately

Misplaced expectations create unnecessary heartbreak.

I learned to stop assigning people roles they never agreed to play. Not everyone in your life is meant to be a champion. Some are companions for a season. Some are encouragers in limited ways. Some are observers, not advocates.

The breakthrough came when I learned to distinguish between someone who *can't* champion me and someone who simply *won't*. That distinction matters. Someone who can't still deserves grace. Someone who won't require boundaries. The way I respond—and the expectations I hold—depends on knowing which one I'm dealing with.

Managing expectations doesn't mean lowering them; it means redirecting them appropriately.

R—Release Personalization

Rejection hits differently when it's silent.

There were moments when the lack of encouragement echoed loudly in my mind. No recommendation. No affirmation. No small push when I needed it. I questioned myself: *Am I asking for too much? Am I not as capable as I thought? Is there something they see that I don't?*

Eventually, I realized that silence does not always point to inadequacy—it often points to misalignment. People enter our lives for different reasons and seasons. Some walk with us for a distance. Others for a moment. A few for the long road.

When I stopped personalizing every "no," clarity replaced confusion. A closed door began to feel less like rejection and more like redirection. Releasing personalization protected my confidence and conserved my emotional energy for relationships that were life-giving.

E—Empower Yourself

When champions didn't show up, I discovered something powerful: I could be my own advocate.

I learned to speak up for myself, correct misunderstandings, and stand tall in rooms where no one was there to vouch for me. I stopped downplaying my achievements. I stopped apologizing for wanting more. And most importantly, I stopped waiting for familiar faces to validate what I already knew about myself.

Letting go of misplaced expectations didn't make me bitter—it made me free. Free to welcome new connections. Free to recognize true champions when they appear. Free to trust myself. That inner shift built a quiet strength—the kind that carries you forward even when you're standing alone.

This is often where real champions are born: in the moments when you choose yourself with clarity and courage.

Getting Over the Disappointment of "No"

There is a unique heartbreak in watching someone step back instead of stepping up. It isn't loud or dramatic—it's subtle. But rising changes perspective. As you grow, you sometimes see limitations in others that were previously invisible.

"No" taught me flexibility. It taught me resilience. It taught me independence rooted in self-trust rather than approval. Over time, "no" became less of a wound and more of a filter. It didn't shut down my future—it protected it.

Why Some People Can't, or Won't Champion You

Not everyone has the capacity to uplift another person. Some are too familiar with who you used to be. Some lack emotional generosity. Some are unstable in their own journey. Others feel intimidated—not by you, but by what your growth forces them to confront in themselves. And some relationships simply lack alignment.

Accepting these truths freed me from chasing validation where it was never going to grow. Support does not need to come from familiar faces to be meaningful. When expectations are aligned with reality, resentment fades, disappointment loosens its grip, and space opens for healthier, more sustainable connections.

Managing expectations is not about lowering standards—it's about aligning hope with wisdom. When you clarify capacity, assign roles accurately, release personalization, and empower yourself, relationships are no longer heavy. They are honest. And from that honesty, freedom grows.

CHAPTER 20

FAMOUS CHAMPIONS WHO CHANGED THE GAME FOR OTHERS

Let me introduce you to a few of the most compelling champions I've studied and admired over the years. These aren't champions because of fame alone. They're champions because they made a deliberate choice to use what they had, platform, money, influence, access, or simply compassion, to lift someone else at a pivotal moment.

What moves me most about these stories is their intentionality. It wasn't for the spotlight. No expectation of recognition. No guarantee that the investment would ever pay off. These individuals understood something profound: when you have a seat at the table, one of the most powerful acts of leadership is pulling out a chair for someone who may not even know the table exists yet.

The champions that follow remind us that changing someone's life rarely requires grand gestures. Sometimes it requires a single decision, made privately, rooted in belief rather than certainty.

Denzel Washington: The Quiet Check That Launched a Legacy

When I first read about the connection between Denzel Washington and Chadwick Boseman, I remember thinking, this is what championing looks like when no one is watching.

In 2003, Chadwick Boseman was a young actor in New York, talented and driven but financially stretched thin. He had been accepted into the Oxford Mid-Summer Program at the British American Drama Academy, an opportunity that could sharpen his craft and expand his future. The only problem was the cost. Tuition was roughly $7,000, and Chadwick simply didn't have it. Faced with reality, he prepared to walk away from the opportunity.

That's when Denzel Washington entered the story. Through a mutual connection, Denzel heard about Chadwick's situation. The two men had never met. There was no personal relationship, no obligation, no strategic advantage. Yet Denzel didn't hesitate. He paid the full tuition outright, privately, without any expectations. No announcement. No acknowledgment. Just a simple act of belief paired with decisive action. His message was essentially, "Go." Learn your craft. Chadwick went. He trained. He absorbed everything he could. And over time, that experience became one of many building blocks that shaped the actor the world would later come to know as the one who made us believe Wakanda was a real place!

Years passed. In 2018, Chadwick Boseman stood at the center of a cultural phenomenon as T'Challa in Black Panther. During interviews, he finally shared the story publicly, his voice thick with emotion, as he explained how that early act of generosity made a difference when he needed it most. He spoke about Denzel not as a celebrity but as a champion.

Denzel's response was understated, almost dismissive of praise. He never framed his action as extraordinary. He didn't seek credit. He simply acknowledged it as something he felt called to do. But the truth is, most people wouldn't have done it. Denzel didn't just have the resources; many people do. What set him apart was his willingness to invest in potential without certainty, to believe in someone before success made belief fashionable. That single decision helped position Chadwick to develop his craft, find his voice, and eventually portray a character who reshaped global representation and inspired millions.

Chadwick Boseman passed away in 2020, but his story didn't end there. Before his death, he paid for other young actors to attend training programs, intentionally continuing the cycle of quiet generosity that began with Denzel. One champion created another. That's the true power of championing. You may never see the full impact of your investment. You may never be thanked publicly. But when you choose to believe early, when you choose to act quietly, you set forces in motion that can outlive you.

That's not just kindness. That's leadership, and that's legacy.

Mr. Rogers: The Man Who Championed Every Child's Worth

Fred Rogers was the most consistent champion of children's emotional lives this country has ever known. He never walked into a boardroom or commanded a corner office. He didn't raise his voice or demand attention. His tools were simple: an ordinary cardigan, a calm tone, and a small television neighborhood that welcomed children exactly as they were. And yet, for more than thirty years. I've gone back and watched old episodes as an adult, and they still move me. There's something disarming about the way he looked directly into the camera and spoke to children as if they mattered deeply, because to him, they did.

He said things most adults avoided: "You are special just the way you are." The generation we grow up in often tells children to toughen up, to be quiet, or to get over their feelings. Mr. Rogers offered a different message. He told them their emotions were real, their questions were valid, and their inner world deserved respect. So, the question is, what made his championing so powerful? It was that he never talked down to kids. He didn't dismiss their fears or rush them past pain. He sat with them. He listened. And in doing so, he gave children language for feelings they didn't yet know how to name.

One moment that has always stayed with me is how he addressed divorce on his show in 1970. Divorce rates were rising, and many children were confused, frightened, and quietly blaming themselves. Fred didn't avoid the topic or sanitize it. Instead, he sat on the floor with Officer Clemmons (an African American man who was a regular on the show) and gently explained that families can change, but love doesn't have to disappear. He created space for sadness without judgment, offering reassurance without false promises. He didn't try to fix the pain; he acknowledged it. That was his gift. He validated what children felt at a time when most adults pretended those feelings were too big and too inconvenient to address.

Fred Rogers never fought for fame or recognition. He fought for children who didn't yet have a voice. He championed their emotional well-being in a society that often treated it as an afterthought. Even now, long after his passing, his gentle voice still echoes: championing doesn't require volume or visibility; it requires presence and a steady heart.

Kobe Bryant: The Girl Dad Who Championed Women's Sports

Having grown up playing basketball and in high school before there was a WNBA, one of my favorite champions is Kobe Bryant. Kobe will always be remembered as one of the greatest basketball players of all time, but some of his most meaningful championing happened after he stepped off the court. In retirement, Kobe embraced a new role with the same intensity he brought to the game: being a father, especially a "girl dad."

He poured himself into his daughters' lives, most notably Gianna, Gigi, who shared his love for basketball. Kobe coached her AAU team, studied film with her, drove carpools, and showed up for games with the same focus he once reserved for championships. He didn't treat youth sports as a hobby. He treated it as an opportunity to teach discipline, confidence, and love for the game. But Kobe's championing extended beyond his own family. He used his influence to elevate women's basketball at a time when it still struggled for recognition and respect. He attended WNBA games and spoke unapologetically about the talent in women's sports. He didn't frame his support as charity. He framed it as truth.

"The game is the game," he often said. "Talent is talent." When players like Sabrina Ionescu began to rise, Kobe was already there, offering guidance and encouragement. He showed up. He listened. He affirmed that excellence doesn't belong to one gender. What made his championing so impactful was consistency. He didn't make a single statement and moved on. He stayed engaged. He invested time. He treated women athletes with the same seriousness and respect he expected for himself.

Kobe didn't just cheer from the sidelines. He built the court. He coached the team. He challenged outdated narratives and made space for girls to see themselves as athletes, leaders, and competitors. His legacy lives on in every young woman who picks up a basketball and feels permission to dream bigger. In every girl who knows she belongs on the court. In every athlete who believes that someone like Kobe saw their worth and said, "You matter here."

That is championing at its best: turning influence into access, belief into action, and legacy into a ladder for the next generation.

Melinda Gates: A Quiet Force Behind Global Change

Another powerhouse who champions others quietly is Melinda Gates. She is not loud about her leadership or philanthropy. She doesn't rely on spectacle or social media sound bites. She works patiently, deliberately, and with an eye toward long-term impact. Through the Bill & Melinda Gates Foundation, she has become one of the most influential champions of women and girls across the globe, often in places where opportunity has never been evenly distributed. What distinguishes her championing is clarity. She recognized early that poverty, health crises, and lack of education disproportionately affect women. Instead of addressing symptoms, she focused on systems, contraception access, maternal health, and education, knowing that when women are empowered, entire communities stabilize and grow.

One story that stands out comes from Ethiopia, where the foundation supported the expansion of community health workers into remote villages. These women brought family planning services and health education directly to households that had never had access before. Melinda didn't limit her involvement to funding alone.

She visited the villages, listened to women describe their lives and limitations, and then used her influence to support policy changes that gave them real choices. Her championing wasn't theoretical; it was rooted in proximity, listening, and action. Beyond global health, Melinda has been a consistent promoter for women in leadership, technology, and politics. After leaving Microsoft, she could have easily stepped back into a quieter philanthropic role. Instead, she launched Pivotal Ventures, an organization designed to fund women-led businesses, support women running for office, and dismantle structural barriers that keep women out of decision-making spaces. She has said plainly, "We need more women in rooms where decisions are made." And then she backed those words with influence and sustained commitment. Melinda Gates champions without urgency for applause. Her work is strategic, long-term, and quietly transformative. She clears paths that women didn't know were possible and often won't realize existed until they're already walking them. That kind of championing doesn't fade when headlines move on. It reshapes futures.

Princess Diana: The People's Champion Who Touched the Untouchable

Princess Diana was born into royalty, but her deepest allegiance was always to those society overlooked. She didn't just symbolize compassion; she practiced it. Again and again, she chose proximity over protocol, presence over image. She walked through active minefields in Angola to bring global attention to landmine victims. She sat with homeless individuals on the street, listening to their stories as if they mattered, because to her, they did. And when the world recoiled from people with AIDS, Diana moved toward them. One moment still stands as a turning point in public consciousness. In 1987, Diana visited a London hospital where AIDS patients were isolated and feared. Medical gloves were the norm. Distance was enforced. Diana removed her gloves and held a patient's hand. The image traveled across the world. In a single moment, AIDS stopped being abstract and feared; it became human. That quiet act changed perception more effectively than any speech ever could; she showed their humanity.

Diana didn't champion the marginalized by speaking for them. She championed them by standing with them. She showed the world that dignity is not something you grant from above; it's something you recognize in front of you. Though cameras followed her everywhere (and I do mean everywhere, including her untimely death), her compassion was not performative. It was instinctive. And that made it powerful. She taught us that championing often means crossing invisible boundaries, touching what others avoid, and refusing to let fear determine where empathy ends. It also meant bucking protocol and traditions that were limiting, stuffy, and outdated. Her legacy reminds us that influence becomes meaningful only when it is used to reduce the distance between people.

Sara Blakely: The Self-Made Champion Who Keeps Shaping Others

Perhaps some of you reading are Spanx wearers, as I am! If so, this next champion will be of interest to you. Sara Blakely built Spanx from a $5,000 idea into a global brand, becoming one of the world's youngest self-made female billionaires. from selling fax machines door-to-door to founding Spanx, a billion-dollar brand that changed the way women feel about their clothes. But the achievement she speaks about most isn't financial; it's the responsibility that comes with making it. From the beginning, Sara has been open about failure. She talks about rejection with humor and honesty, often reminding women that failure isn't a stop sign; it's part of the path. Through the Sara Blakely Foundation, she funds women entrepreneurs, mentors founders, and invests in businesses led by women who look a lot like she once did: uncertain, ambitious, and willing to try.

One example of her championing stands out: when the Atlanta Dream WNBA team was struggling, Sara didn't just write a check. She became a part-owner. She attended games. She amplified the players. She used her platform to draw attention to women's sports, understanding that visibility is just as valuable as funding. Her support wasn't symbolic; it was participatory. Sara champions practicality. She gives resources, access, encouragement, and belief. She doesn't separate success from responsibility. She reaches back instinctively, pulling others forward not because she has to, but because she remembers what it felt like to need someone to believe. She is proof that championing doesn't require perfection or polish, just willingness.

What These Champions Teach Us

These champions share no single personality, background, or method. Some worked quietly. Others stood in the public eye. Some used money. Others used presence. But they all lived the same truth: You don't need fame to champion someone. You don't need fortune. You need vision, the ability to see potential where others see limitations. You need compassion, the willingness to care without conditions, and the courage, the readiness to act when it would be easier not to. It also teaches us the power of ownership. They don't just do a job; they own it. They learn their craft deeply. They refine it. They redefine what excellence looks like. They don't wait to be managed into greatness; they take responsibility for the quality of their work. Champions exceed expectations because they set higher ones for themselves.

This kind of championship doesn't belong only to athletes, executives, or public figures. That definition is far too narrow. A single mother working two jobs to keep food on the table and the lights on is a champion. She adapts, perseveres, and sacrifices daily. She manages exhaustion, pressure, and responsibility with little margin for error. She does whatever it takes to keep moving forward. That is a championship in its truest form. Champions teach us that winning isn't always visible. Sometimes it looks like resilience. Sometimes it looks like consistency. Sometimes it looks like getting up one more time when quitting would be easier. We need champions because they expand our understanding of what's possible. Seeing someone push through a limitation, whether external or internal, reshapes our own thinking. Their example quietly asks the question. What if I didn't quit? What if I tried again? What if I stayed the course and allowed someone to mention my name in rooms I have yet to enter? What if I can be successful? Champions help us understand the answer to those unspoken questions, and they give us the courage to find out.

CHAPTER 21

HOW TO SECURE A CHAMPION

Let's pause here for a moment, because this is usually the question people lean forward for: How do I actually get a champion in my corner? I wish I could hand you a perfect script, a clever email, or some secret professional shortcut. But the truth is simpler and harder than that. Champions aren't recruited. They aren't convinced. They choose you because, over time, you've made it clear that betting on you makes sense. This isn't theory. It's what I've watched unfold in my own life and in the lives of people I deeply respect.

The first and most important step is to truly master what you do. Quiet excellence naturally makes a positive impression and tends to precede you, opening doors and inspiring confidence in you. When your work consistently speaks for itself, people start noticing, even when you're not in the room. Early in my career, I spent countless hours grinding through financial reports that no one outside my department was ever supposed to see. Still, I treated every spreadsheet as if it were going straight to the boardroom. One day, a senior leader from another division reviewed one of those reports and asked, "Who put this together?" My boss said my name. "Andrea Humphrey." He didn't know my ambitions or my long-term plans; he knew my work. And that was enough. Excellence is often the first introduction you'll ever make to a future champion. But excellence alone isn't enough if it isn't consistent. Champions look for reliability. Show up the same way every day, prepared and professional. Be clear about what you do and how you do it. Avoid unnecessary drama. Stay out of gossip. Own mistakes quickly. This point I found is important in being trusted, not to be perfect, but integral. While working for Walt Disney Imagineering, I once made a huge mistake on a project that was the hottest new addition to the parks. I had been working late into the night to get numbers to the Vice President of the portfolio by 8:00 am. I left the office at 1:30 am and returned at 7:00 to finish up. In my tired haste, I omitted a critical piece of the budget, and it was only discovered after it had been sent to corporate for approval. I had to go and tell the VP that the numbers were wrong, and in so doing, the thought that I could lose my job was squarely on my mind. I approached the mistake with honesty and humility, took responsibility, and let him know that I would go to corporate and let them know it was my fault. Although he was upset, he noticed the timestamp on the document and asked if I had printed it out at 1:30 in the morning. I told him yes, it was true, and he then said that having worked that many hours straight, it could have happened to anyone who was tired and had been crunching numbers for 17 hours straight. He thanked me for my honesty and became one of my biggest champions and was responsible for my next two promotions.

Integrity and consistency are critical for people to champion you. I've seen incredibly talented people miss opportunities for promotable assignments simply because they were unpredictable. Brilliant one day, absent the next. Champions place their reputation on the line when they support you. They want to know you'll show up when it counts. You also must learn how to encourage yourself, calmly and respectfully. For a long time, I believed that if I worked hard enough, someone would notice. Eventually, I realized that no one is assigned to manage my career but me. That's when I started sharing short, thoughtful updates with leaders I admired: what I'd accomplished, what I'd learned, where I wanted to stretch next. Not bragging, just visibility. Champions can't support someone they don't know exists. You don't need to shout. You just need to be seen.

Another quality champions pay close attention to is coachability. Nothing shuts a door faster than someone who believes they already have all the answers. When feedback comes, and it will, listen. Thank the person. Apply what you've been given. Some of the most valuable advice I've received was uncomfortable in the moment, but I chose to learn from it were uncomfortable in the moment, but I chose to learn from them rather than defend myself. Champions notice that. Coachability tells them their time, energy, and belief won't be wasted.

Gratitude and humility matter more than people realize. Say thank you often. Acknowledge support. Celebrate the success of the people who help you along the way. Humility isn't shrinking yourself; it's recognizing that you didn't get where you are alone. Champions are usually carrying a lot already. When you respect their time and honor their investment, they're far more inclined to continue showing up for you. When a champion gives you an opportunity, especially a small one, treat it like it matters, because it does. If they introduce you to someone, follow up well. If they offer you a project, exceed expectations. If they give you a chance to speak, prepare like it's the biggest room you've ever been in. I once stepped in to cover for a speaker at the last minute. I prepared like my future depended on it, because in many ways, it did. The response opened doors I couldn't have planned for. Champions watch how you handle what seems minor before trusting you with something major.

Champion relationships will be built strongly and long before you follow these things. Invest in people. Show up to their events. Read their work. Send a note when something they shared resonated with you. Offer help without keeping score. Trust grows slowly, through proximity and consistency. Champions rarely emerge from cold outreach. They come from warm, real relationships. And finally, don't be afraid to ask. This part took me time. Asking felt risky. But once you've done the work, asking isn't entitlement; it's clarity. I've learned to say things like, "I admire the way you've built your career, and I'm working toward something similar. Would you be open to coffee sometime?" Or "I'm ready for a bigger stretch. If something crosses your desk that feels aligned, would you think of me?" Sometimes the answer is no. Sometimes it's not yet. And sometimes, it's exactly the opening you needed. Securing a champion isn't about manipulation or clever networking. It's about becoming someone others are proud to stand behind. Do your work well. Show up consistently. Stay teachable. Treat people generously. When you live that way, champions don't appear overnight, but they do appear. They've been watching longer than you realize. And when they decide to step forward, they'll use their influence to make space for you at the table. That's how it works.

Being a Champion for Others

Here is the truth that matters most in this work: the greatest reward isn't just finding a champion—it's becoming one. At some point, the focus shifts. You stop asking, *"Who is going to open the door for me?"* and you start asking, *"Whose door can I open?"*—that is when success stops being about progress and starts being about purpose.

I believe this with everything in me: be the thing you once prayed for. If you can remember a season when you felt stuck, overlooked, or quietly questioning whether anyone truly saw your potential, don't forget that feeling. Let it guide you. Then go find someone carrying that same weight and help lighten it. For a long time, I believed championing others was something you did after you "made it." But I learned you don't have to be at the top to reach back. You can start exactly where you are.

The moment someone championed me, something shifted internally. I stopped guarding opportunities like they were scarce and started sharing them like they were meant to circulate. I realized how powerful it is to be the open door you once hoped someone would knock on. We love the idea of pulling ourselves up by our bootstraps, but the truth is, that story is incomplete. Every successful person I know can name someone who spoke up for them, made an introduction, took a chance, or offered guidance at the right moment.

When I look at my own journey—from moving from Northrop to Disney because a former coworker advocated for me to teaching women around the world because Tyran Meredith and Dr. Pat Bailey chose to bring me along—I know I didn't get there alone. And once you see that clearly, you can't unsee it. You stop letting others struggle in isolation when you have the ability to help.

Being a champion doesn't mean lifting everyone; it means choosing wisely. Look for people who are growing, hungry, and coachable. Start with those whose curiosity and effort remind you of your younger self—the professional who asks thoughtful questions, the single mother taking one class at a time, the teenager stepping into leadership before they feel ready. Pay attention to humility, work ethic, and heart. I'm drawn to people who are already moving forward. I don't need to carry them; I just want to add a little wind to their sails.

And here's what people often underestimate: affirmation costs almost nothing, but it can mean everything. A text that says, "I noticed your work—well done." A public acknowledgment in a meeting. A handwritten note that says, "I believe in you." I have watched posture change, confidence rise, and hope return because of one sincere sentence. Most people are quietly hoping someone sees that they're trying. Be the one who says it out loud.

Investing in the next generation matters deeply to me. I think about my daughters and the young women I've mentored over the years. We carry wisdom that was hard-earned and expensive. Giving it away costs us nothing. Share the shortcuts you learned the long way. Warn them about mistakes you wish you'd avoided. Celebrate their wins like they're your own. I've taken young speakers under my wing, helped shape their messages, made introductions, and watched them soar beyond anything I imagined for myself. There is a special joy in helping someone else build something meaningful.

Your life changes when you help change someone else's. I felt it the first time a young woman I mentored landed her dream job because I made one phone call. I felt it again years later when a teenager told me my encouragement kept her from quitting school. That kind of impact heals old wounds you didn't realize you were still carrying. It reframes your struggles as part of a larger purpose.

I can't close this chapter without sharing a story that perfectly illustrates the power of championing one another and how sometimes, championing comes full circle.

Sherri Shepherd has been a supporter of my work for years, and I have always made it a priority to encourage her, pray for her, and support her in any way I can. A few years ago, while she was visiting, she casually mentioned that she might be getting her own talk show after her time on *The View*. I was genuinely thrilled for her. I knew without question that she would be incredible—her humor, charisma, and authenticity practically guarantee success.

Not long after, Sherri did, in fact, get her own show. As soon as I heard, I knew I wanted to be there to support her in person. I decided to surprise her, so I didn't say a word about my plans. As it turned out, I was seated on the end of a row where she would eventually walk during the audience interaction portion of the show.

At the end of the taping, she came up my row, speaking to an audience member with her back to me. As she turned to head back toward the stage, I casually said, "Hey lady."

She froze, turned around, recognized my voice, and immediately screamed, "Hey Dr. Dre! What are you doing here?" laughing and grinning from ear to ear.

I told her I had come to support her.

She had to step away briefly for a commercial break, but when she returned, she motioned for me to come down near the camera. Right there, live on air, she shouted me out and highlighted the work I do. In that moment, she became a champion for me—publicly, generously, and without hesitation.

I had come to cheer her on, and she turned around and championed me.

That is where the power of the four C's truly comes alive. It's not just about building a team that builds you—it's about building people. When you genuinely lift others, support their calling, and celebrate their wins, it has a way of returning to you in unexpected and powerful ways.

That is the legacy I want to leave on the earth: championing as many people as I can, trusting that what you sow, you will reap.

Because legacy isn't built on accomplishments alone.

Titles fade. Awards fade. Platforms fade.

Influence remains.

When I'm gone, I don't want to be remembered for the parks I helped build at Disney or the countries I taught in. I want to be remembered by the people who say, *"Andrea saw something in me and wouldn't let me quit."*

That is the kind of legacy that keeps moving long after you're done.

I've watched my husband live this out beautifully. He once recommended a gifted friend for a role, fully aware that the man might outshine him—and he did. Eventually, that friend became his boss. But my husband never felt threatened. He felt proud. Their relationship deepened because the door was opened without fear.

Become the champion you once needed. Watch what happens to them. Then watch what happens to you. Once you live this way, you'll never want to live any other way again.

CHAPTER 22

A FINAL THOUGHT

Cheerleaders, coaches, comrades, and champions—we need all of them at different points in our lives. Over the course of a lifetime, we may have several of each. Building the team that builds you is critical to bringing out the best in you and positioning you to operate at your optimal potential, even when you cannot yet see the full height of that potential for yourself.

Throughout this book, I've shared frameworks and insights drawn from my work as a leadership specialist, speaker, and author. I should also share that I am a pastor. While this is not a Christian book, I would be remiss if I did not offer one closing reflection because my own journey of leadership and success has often unfolded during seasons when some of these pillars were not present in human form.

Whether you believe as I do is, of course, your prerogative. My intention is not to persuade, but to invite you to consider this: if you ever find yourself in need of a cheerleader when encouragement is scarce; a coach when wisdom and direction feel out of reach; a comrade when companionship is missing; or a champion when no one seems willing to open a door or pull out a seat at the table God is able and willing to be all of those things.

For more than forty years, I have leaned on the Creator, and I have never been left without wisdom, insight, help, or encouragement. When human support was unavailable or insufficient, divine presence proved consistent. Go ahead and build the team that builds you and watch the shift in your career, relationships, and personal life flourish.

So, if you find yourself in a season where one or more of these pillars is missing, and no person seems able to fill the gap, I encourage you to pause if only for a moment and whisper a prayer. Ask God for help. You may be surprised by how He shows up, and by how He proves Himself to be the most faithful, most present, most powerful, and most generous Cheerleader, Coach, Comrade, and the ultimate Champion.

Start today, building the team that builds you, you deserve to operate your very best!

www.ingramcontent.com/pod-product-compliance
Lightning Source LLC
Chambersburg PA
CBHW051246050726
47594CB00001B/325